NO MORE
MR. CHAI GUY

No More Mr. Chai Guy

© copyright 2024 J.P. Sterling

Editors: Rebecca Carpenter and Brenda Bastien

All right reserved. No part of this book may be reproduced or transmitted in any form or by any means, audio, electronic or mechanical, including photocopying, recording, or by any information storage and retrieval system, without permission in writing from the publisher.

This is a work of fiction. Any mention of names, places, and characters is fiction and for entertainment purposes only.

Warning: the unauthorized reproduction or distribution of this copyrighted work is illegal. Copyright infringement, including infringement without monetary gain, is a criminal offense.

Not liable for any sudden coffee cravings which occur while reading this book.

Contents

Blurb

An All-Star football player. A popular cheerleader. Can they finally move from the friend zone to the end zone?

Gia Bella

I've been working this low-wage-going-nowhere job for ten years. Don't even ask about my dating life. Yes, sir, life is pretty...uneventful. That is until my hoarding dad accidentally burrito-wraps himself in his collection of fly paper.

I'll pause so you can visualize that.

Who should answer his bellowing cries for help, but none other than the boy next door—A.K.A. North Newson, the single man I've loved since I was six years old. Only now, he's all grown up, and still oh so handsome.

With decades of unrequited love steeping, I can't fight the attraction anymore.

However, there's one small issue.

Just when we make progress, he pulls away as he did last time, leaving me to wonder if he's falling for me too, or if he's just simply being a nice guy.

North Newson

Highschool was football and Gia, but life brought about one giant fumble for both.

I moved on from football, going to college for coaching instead. I lucked out and scored the head coaching job at the very same school I had attended. But I never moved on from Gia no matter how hard I tried. When a second chance with Gia shows up, the instant magnetism returns, and I try my hardest to win her heart.

However, there's one small issue.

Someone is trying to keep us apart . . . but I won't be defeated again.

No More Mr. Chai Guy is a 2nd chance, Brother's rival, sweet romcom with a HEA.

ONE

Gia Bella

Homecoming Game

A rush of adrenaline fuels my heart to thump out like thunderclaps as I weave in between the support beams of the old rickety bleachers. It's junior year Homecoming, and I'm finally an upper classman. I'm determined to make this year the best year—and one to remember forever. Our mediocre-and-a-tad-squeaky marching band has begun to practice the school's fight song for the half-time performance, and the disjointed melodies fill the crisp autumn air. The anticipation of the year's most exciting event already hangs thick as fans trickle in.

Here I am squinting—I lost a contact lens in cheerleading practice—until my eyes land on him.

North Newson.

The single soul I've been enamored with since I first laid eyes on him. With a deep breath, I pool all my courage, and continue towards him, heart pounding against my rib cage.

North is so handsome he makes people around him halt in their tracks. Being humble, he returns my gaze with a nonchalant smile and shy wave, but I can't imagine he doesn't know what his presence does to all the girls. The flush of his cheeks gives away his true feelings as more than modesty. He is one thousand percent shy, but that only makes all the girls fawn over him more. Despite his many options—any girl he'd want—he remains single, adding to the mystery.

Oh, and he's in the senior class with my older brother, Rocco, and happens to live right next door, so I see an awful lot of North.

Not that I'm complaining.

Nope, nothing but positive vibes from me.

Maybe a little blushing.

I was six years old when we moved into our little rambler next door to him. The drive from east Long Island wasn't long, but I had packed all my stuffed animals in the backseat in between Rocco and me. Of course, Rocco grumbled about them, but I tuned him out by sticking a Hello Kitty earbud into each ear. When Dad pulled our Dodge minivan into our desperately-needing-some cement-patches driveway, I had loaded as many stuffies as I could carry in my arms—with no help from Rocco.

Being independent for a grade schooler, I had planned for a second trip. When I returned for them, North stood with the rest of my stuffies. He had watched us pull in from his picture window and had run over to help. With his wild dark mop of hair that curled by his ears, and the perfect shade of naturally-sun-kissed olive skin, I had decided then and there that he was the most beautiful boy I'd ever seen.

Ever since football season started, we've been secretly meeting under the bleachers before the games. It began as a cheerleading thing, as my squad had put together treat bags for each player, filled with a sports drink, protein bars, and cards we all signed. I begged my squad to let me personally give North his bag, and then he started asking to meet in the same spot each week. He claims I'm good luck. Last week he even brought me a blue carnation.

What in the world of flower language does blue mean?

He said it was Bulldog blue. Our school colors are red, white, and blue, but I'm not going to lie, I hope it means he loves me. I don't want to be that pick-me girl that people complain about but when it comes to North, yes, I'm her.

Being so shy, he didn't say much about the flower other than, "It's for good luck." I didn't care if it was for horrible luck, I accepted that flower, and when it started to die, I pressed it in my chemistry book.

My heart pumps against my ribcage. The mystery of this meet-up and the excitement of my crush swirl together. "Hey Gia." The light wind rustles the lush curls by his ears. He's already wearing his #47 Bulldog jersey, complete with eye black, while he cradles his helmet under his arm. My heart could literally skip an entire chorus of beats just to hear him say my name.

"Hey." I do my best to act chill, and flash him my cool smile. "How are you?"

"I can't believe it's my last Homecoming game." He shifts the helmet from one arm to the other. "I guess I got the warmup time wrong, and I only have a few minutes." Pausing, he scratches an itch on the back of his head and speaks even slower, "Ah, earlier I overheard Rocco mention you didn't have a date for the dance tonight." His gaze dips to his feet before raising back up to lock on me, and his words rush out, "Would you save me a dance later?"

A ping slams into my heart, almost breaking my balance. I grab onto the bleacher support beam and pray this isn't the day these ancient poles decide to disintegrate into the ground.

I nervously twirl the end of my long ponytail with my free hand and pause, desperate not to look too eager. Then a weird thought enters my mind.

Why only one dance?

Is he asking me because he feels bad that I don't have a date? Why would he not ask me to be his date? The mere thought of me being his date, dancing in his arms, makes my blood pressure skyrocket.

His deep, espresso eyes dig into mine as he waits for an answer. Those eyes do nothing to lower my blood pressure, and my breathing ticks up another notch as I fight the steady slams of my heart headbutting my ribs. If he keeps staring at me like that, I'm going to need a paper bag to breathe in. There's nobody else I'd rather dance with. "I'd like that," I say softly, before lowering my lashes and smiling sweetly.

"Cool," he quips, and jerks his head toward the locker room. "I better go. I'll look for you later."

"Same." Suppressing a squeal, I nibble on my bottom lip and wave as he turns to leave. This night is going to be magical, just like I knew this whole year would be.

Two

North Newson

"I'm open!" My throat burns with hot breath as I emit a scream that formed from the bottom of my gut. I weave to dodge defensive player #22. Our star running back, Rocco Bella, hurls a long pass at me. I lunge forward, grappling for the football, barely staying upright, if not for the tips of my toes. Once I regain my footing, I'm gone.

Destination: endzone.

"Ladies and gentlemen," the announcer's voice ticks up in tension, running back #47, North Newson, has the ball, and he's heading to the endzone!" The crowd rushes to their feet with fanatical screaming. I pump my legs faster while the announcer echoes over the speakers. "Forty yards, he's going for it!"

I'm lightning, but my immediate goal is to be even faster. I dig in and pull as much speed as I can. This touchdown is all we need to take the lead, and we are down to two minutes on the clock. I don't even want to think about the scout in the stands tonight who made it clear he was watching both Rocco and me. It's both of our goals to play in the NFL, and winning this game could make both our dreams come true. "Thirty yards!" the announcer counts down, his voice on edge. The crowd becomes unhinged.

A linebacker's behind me now. He's so close, his breath puffs out in audible waves, which make the hairs on the back of my neck stand up. My chest drums out explosions, as my heart crawls into my throat and I top out my speed. I'm almost there. Twenty more yards.

Cramps snake up my calves, begging me to slow down, but my mind is a tank, and I refuse to cave to any pain.

The linebacker finds a burst of speed, rushing my side, but I'm slick and weave to the side, dodging him. The crowd rumbles with so much noise, it's as if the bleachers are about to collapse, and the ground is going to split open. The linebacker isn't done, and he is back on my side again. There's nowhere for me to go! I'm blazing forward and being run out of bounds.

There's someone here!

A cheerleader in mid-cheer.

I frantically swipe my hand to push her out of the way, but she's not paying attention and *wham*! We collide. I tumble over her, taking her with me, and we roll together off the field all the while the crowd is roaring.

When we finally stop turning, I steal my gaze forward. I'm laying smack on top of Gia Bella.

Head cheerleader.

Prettiest girl in school.

Rocco's little sister.

She also just happens to be the woman I've been secretly in love with for *years*.

Her gaze hooks mine, and our breaths heave out, blending as we freeze together by instant magnetism.

"North! Nice job throwing the game for us," Rocco sarcastically screams as he jogs to the sidelines, anger oozing out of his eyes. "And get off my sister!"

Ice pumps through my veins as my body awakens to the fact that *I'm lying on top of Gia Bella*! I quickly roll off her, face fiery with embarrassment, and I pray we can laugh this whole thing off. As I rush to my feet, I reach back to offer Gia a hand up, but her face pinches and she grabs her knee.

The crowd quickly hushes, and it's so quiet you can hear a fly fart. "Are you okay?" I whisper as if the sound will cause her more pain.

Her silky ponytail cascades over her shoulder, shielding her face from me, but it doesn't fully conceal her clenching eyes with a single tear drop below the left one.

I suck in a hard breath.

She's hurt.

I did this to her.

I blink, and Rocco slides in next to her, pushing me to fade to the background before I have a chance to plead sorry. She's quickly surrounded by medics. Her dad flies out of the bleachers, huddling in, and then she's whisked off the field. My team's lining up again, but I'm frozen.

"North!" Coach yells at me. "You're benched."

Of course, I am!

At this point I hardly care about the game, as my heart's slamming against my ribcage, panting Gia's name. I want to run after her, but there's nothing I can do for her.

The game must go on.

I regretfully take my seat on the edge of the bench, while my teammates pound my back. "Wrong kind of touchdown, Bruh," someone snickers.

Rocco returns, glaring at me through narrowed eyes, smeared with his eye black, and he grumbles, "You know, you just ruined everything. We were supposed to win tonight."

"How is she?" I rise to my feet, searching his face for clues.

"Stay away from my sister," he growls while piercing his eyes into mine, sending a chill spiraling through them all the way down to my toes.

"It was clearly an accident," My voice is resolute, and I take a solid step back from Rocco. A switch has been flipped, and Rocco's grin widens as he steps closer, closing the gap I had just created, while invading my personal space.

"You better watch your back," he sneers, his breath hot on my face. But as he raises his fist to strike, coach comes out from behind us, freezing us both in place.

"To the bench, boys. *Now!*"

She's fine, I reassure myself, as I pivot, and plop down on the bench, hanging my head. I've taken way worse hits than that and walked them off. She'll be right back out in a few moments. I stare down the path that leads to the locker rooms, waiting.

Please come out and be okay.

But she never returns to the field.

THREE

Gia

I sprawl out in the center of my queen bed, my back propped up on a pile of goose-down pillows with a bag of frozen peas strapped to my puffed knee. *She's All That* plays on the TV again for what seems like the hundredth time. I turn the volume all the way down until the only sound that echoes in my room is the rain outside my window. I flick the remote next to me and wince.

My knee pulses with a heartbeat of its own.

The x-rays showed nothing broken. Thankfully. However, I was mid-cheer with my raised leg bent when the blunt force met my knee, and it dislocated my pelvis. Now I'm stuck home on the night of the biggest dance of the year with a giant stabilizing belt strapped around my hips. My cheer squad all called to express their concern, but they sure didn't slow down their plans on my account. I can't believe I'm missing the Homecoming dance. Not to mention, I didn't get to take North up on that dance I promised him.

That one hurt the most.

For two weeks, I had washed dishes at my dad's pizzeria to earn money for the perfect mermaid-silhouette dress. The stylish garment hangs from the back of my closet door as a taunting reminder—tonight is not going how I had envisioned it. My friends are all at the dance, wearing their dresses. I can almost see them with their hair and makeup done, and dancing with the biggest smiles on their faces. I want to be happy for them, but it stings to think I'm missing out.

Major FOMO.

Worst of all is the nagging thought in the back of my mind that North's dancing with someone else. Clenching my eyes, I gulp another lungful of air and hold it as I struggle through the tears. Junior year is supposed to be one of my best years, but so far this year has been hellacious. One month in and I'm nearly disabled. So much for the cheer team.

What else can go wrong?

A soft knock comes from my bedroom door.

Really? I arch a suspicious brow. I wasn't inviting something else to go wrong. How's this happening?

"What?" My voice drips in nasal-ly inflections, but I don't reach for a tissue. I'm so over everything.

The door pushes open, and I'm expecting my dad, or my brother, but it's neither.

It's North.

My eyes immediately skirt over the dirty cheerleading uniform I'd lazily dropped when I changed. My soggy shower towel still lays mid-center on the floor, as I was too disgruntled to bother to hang it up. It's all so cringe, but I can't even move to try to nonchalantly kick those things under my bed. My eyes bug out of my head as an inventory of all the childish stuffed animals I still had lined up on my dresser runs through my head. Can't a girl get a warning? I force a calm smile and lock my gaze back to him.

That did absolutely nothing to calm my nerves, because while I'm laid up, looking like a spicy disaster, he is killing all the looks categories. He's so tall and fit, he looks like a football model in his letterman jacket, and his tousled hair only makes him look more smoldering, drawing me in like a magnet. My palms are pouring out sweat, my hands growing sticky, as I try to casually wipe them on my blanket all the while my cheeks flush with anticipation.

North is here.

In my room.

To see me.

Of course, this is about what happened. More than likely it's a welfare check, but my heart is already making wedding plans. I can't for a second be mad at him for running into me because it was an accident. His brow lowers as his gaze glides from my pea-encapsulated knee back up to my face. "I'm sorry, Gia. I honestly didn't see you there until it was too late."

"It's okay." I sigh, hoping I will be okay.

"Rocco said nothing is broken." His athletic-build shoulders fall, as if he is giving himself permission to let go of his own anxiety. I find myself staring at them. If things had been different tonight, I would be at the dance with my arms wrapped around those brawny shoulders, spinning around the dance floor...

Heat creeps over my cheeks and I blink my way back into this conversation. "Nope. Nothing is broken. I get to rest a lot and start some physical therapy." It's never hard to form a sweet smile for him. His eyes are so wide with concern, molten honey hues sparkle out of the center like the deepest espresso. They are more decadent than a morsel of the most desired candy, and all I want to do is study them until I have a Ph.D. in his eyes. I struggle not to blurt out how handsome he is. "I'm going to be fine."

He stuffs his hands in his letterman jacket pockets and rocks back on his heels. Need I comment on how doing something as simple as that makes him that much hotter? Anything he does adds another layer of handsomeness to him. He's clearly won the gene pool lottery for every feature of his face, but the fact that he's humble about it magnifies his handsomeness by a billion. "I, ah, brought you something."

My head springs back, and I give him another quick once over. He's not holding anything. "You did?"

"Yeah, I left it in the hall because I wanted to check on you first." He sticks one of his Nike sneakers back out the door, before softly calling back, "I wanted to make sure you were awake first." When he pops his head back in, he's got a half-crooked smile on his face—the one all the girls talk about—and he's carrying a *toddler-sized*, reptilian, stuffed animal. It's bubblegum pink with three horns sticking out on each side of its head. He has an open mouth grin on his face, he's literally the cutest lizard I've ever seen. "I hope you still like stuffed animals."

The memory of our first meeting slams into my brain, and my cheeks rage with fire. I can't believe he still remembers. And yes, I'm still obsessed with stuffed animals, even though I'm supposed to be past that age. I'm stunned into silence, rapidly blinking to see if I'd somehow opened my eyes to an alternate reality. One where this isn't happening, because this doesn't happen to me. I take the stuffie into my arms and squeeze him tightly as if this alone has the power to heal me. He takes up my whole lap, but I don't set him next to me. I can't stop holding him. It's comforting to have something weighty on me.

"It's an axolotl," North is now standing so close to my bed, I can smell his deodorant. It's like miles of evergreen forest doused in rainwater, mixed with the embers from a recent campfire. I've never yearned to be a Girl Scout more in my life. I blink, forcing myself out of my distraction, *again*, North is still talking, "—a special type of salamander who's endangered. They make the best pets because they always look happy, and my goal is to get a real one someday."

I cling to my stuffie, peering at North over his adorable head, the kindness of his gift sweeping into my heart with the speed of a desert windstorm. I really didn't hear more than a few words about his weird amphibian hobby, but I had never been more ecstatic to pretend to care about something boring. "That's awfully sweet of you, and so fascinating." I bat my lashes, and I continue to gush. "I saw you skip lunch a few times for the science Olympiad, but I didn't know you were such a fan of lizards."

"What's not to love?" He gives me a masculine one-shoulder shrug before tacking on, "I was hoping he'd make you smile."

"Thank you." Despite my knee pulsating like a strobe light, my lips are about to crack down the center as I'm beaming brighter than a spotlight. After a pause, I force a change of subject, "How was the dance?"

"Ah, I never made it there. I was worried about you."

"Oh." A magnified ping—that was more like a clang of cymbals—vibrates in my gut. I hadn't considered North's visit to be anything more than an obligation to clear the air. The dance is the biggest event in school and everybody and their dog goes. My voice is tiny, as if afraid to mingle with the air when I echo, "You didn't want to go to the dance?"

"Nah." He passes his hand through his hair, ruffling it even more. "The only reason I wanted to go in the first place was to get a chance to dance with you, but since I ruined that, there was no reason for me to go."

My eyes skirt my room. He really is here to see *me.* He could easily have sent the stuffed animal home with Rocco if he had wanted to go out, but he didn't.

He came here.

The hottest guy skipped the biggest dance of the year to see me. That means something, right? If I had known that blowing my knee would summon the hottest boy in school over to my bedroom, I'd have hired my own hitman.

My heart motors against my ribcage as I take a risk and motion to my desk chair. "Did you want to hang out? I can put something better on the TV."

"Yeah, I would." He glances down at his Nikes for a split second, before bringing his gaze back up, his beautiful eyes trapping mine. "I ah, actually, am, wondering if maybe sometime, you'd—"

"Gia!" My dad manifests in my doorway behind North, holding a plate up near his ear like the perfect waiter. I love my dad, but I want to shoot daggers out my eyes at him as he has the worst timing. Could he not have eavesdropped first to find out we were about to have a moment! "Pizza's here." Dad gestures to the plate he's holding, as if nobody on the planet has ever seen one of those. Of course it's pizza. It's clearly not a chicken. Add to the fact that dad *always* has a pizza.

He's owned a pizzeria called Bella's—named after our last name—since he was fresh out of school. He always jokes that since my mom died, pizza is his one true love, and the only thing he knows how to cook. He's not a man of many words, but he loves to use food as a point of connection, and this is clearly his way of cheering me up.

"Hi, Mr. Bella," North bleeps as he straightens his posture and darts his hand through his hair again.

"It was a good game." Dad obviously ignores the bigger issue as he pats North on the back with his free hand. "We almost had them." Another one of Dad's loves is football. North is clearly a third. He has a heart for many things, and he's never been one to hold a grudge. He also isn't one of those overbearing dads. He's the dad who effortlessly smooths everything out. "Did you see they patched Gia back together?"

"Yeah." North's dimpled chin moves up and down, fire on his cheeks. "I'm so sorry for all the trouble I caused."

"Not your fault. Accidents happen." Dad gently waves off North's apology. "There's plenty more pizza in the kitchen. Go back and help yourself. I brought extra home so the kids can stop over to eat after the dance."

North's gaze bounces back to me, and then on Dad. "Ah, I—"

"Grab a slice and bring it back." Dad jerks a thumb over his shoulder toward the kitchen. "Gia's not going any-where." Dad advances to the chair I had moments earlier offered North, and plops down. "I'm here, too. We can all hang out."

"Th-thank you." North stammers before scurrying down the hall. Dad slides my plate over to me, his gaze snagging on the axolotl. "Did North bring you that?"

I nod, as I blot the top layer of grease off my pizza with a napkin Dad had tucked under my slice. I've never kept any secrets from dad as we had a very open and chatty relationship.

While scratching his neck, Dad stares back to the empty hall. "That boy has always had a serious case of puppy love for you."

"—Dad!" My cheeks glow warm as I rush to cut him off in a hushed voice. "He can *hear* you."

"Nothing wrong with what I'm saying. He's a nice guy. Just too shy. He needs to get over it and just come out and tell everyone how he feels about you."

My gaze slides to my knee. "He said he feels awful."

"I wasn't talking about your knee." Dad scoffs as North's footsteps return in the hall, but he doesn't shut up. "We all know there's more going on in that boy's head than feeling awful."

Dad's words drop off right as North returns, and an echo reverberates in the room. I fight the urge to crawl under my blanket. I love my dad dearly, but some days he's so cringe. "Come on in." Dad's boisterous voice fills in the pulsating silence, and I suffer through the next twenty minutes of listening to him tell North all about the new mixer he got at the pizzeria. North's a good sport and doesn't let a stray eye linger my way as he stays glued to dad's every word, leaving me to wonder if it will ever be my turn to talk to North.

Truthfully, it's very unlikely as he just seems so shy about some things. The fact that he came here at all is really a miracle.

Four

North

My lower back is a bay of sweat by the time I finally find a long enough pause in Mr. Bella's pizzeria stories to excuse myself for the night. He's alright for a dad, and all, but I get the impression that he's suspicious of me, like he can tell how much I care about Gia.

Maybe I'm overreacting.

I hope I'm overreacting.

With a cringe on my face, I tiptoe down the hall at record speeds, ready to make a clean break. It's apparently not my night as I nearly smack into Rocco, who is coming through the kitchen side door. His eyes immediately narrow, skipping over me to bounce on Gia's open bedroom door then dart back to me. "Sup, Bruh?'

"Nothing." I rub the back of my neck, forcing myself to appear casual. "Just stopped over to see how Gia is doing."

"It's almost midnight."

"Right." Standing my ground, I jerk a thumb over my shoulder back toward her room. "Dude, your dad's been here the whole time, feeding us pizza. He had all these stories, and I thought it was rude to leave."

"Are you for real?" He steps forward, his nostrils flaring out like he's sniffing me. Even though he plays running back, the dude's built like a linebacker. But it doesn't matter if he's built like a ballerina, he's not a dude you want in your face. "What do you have going on with my sister?"

"Nothing." I clamp my mouth shut and wag my head, totally confused he'd care this much. Before I know it, his fist finds my jacket collar, and he slams me against the wall. "I'm only going to tell you one more time. You stay away from her, or else."

"—Ah, or else." I scramble to find my footing, and slide against the wall, inching toward the door. I know giving into his taunts will only make it worse, but I really have no intentions of fighting him. I'd rather just walk away.

"Just stay away from her," he hisses right as Mr. Bella appears in the hall.

Finally, one time Mr. Bella's magical manifesting power helps me out. "I thought I heard someone out here. How was the dance, Rocco?"

"Fine." Rocco's dark eyes never leave my face, and he takes another step, crowding me toward the door. "Just seeing North out."

"R-right," I stammer, as the doorknob is finally in reach, and I toss a wave over my shoulder. "Bye, Mr. Bella. See you later, Rocco."

I'm out the door in the next second, slamming it behind me to race across the yard. I have no idea what got into Rocco. He's never been that way with me before, but apparently, he's protective of his sister.

I don't ever want to see that side of him again.

Five

The next Friday night, dad picks me up from school, but since he has to close the pizzeria, he takes me back with him. We sit in my favorite booth, the one with the red stained-glass tiffany lamp hanging above it, and a black and white photo of the Brooklyn Bridge next to the large window. Rocco—along with all my cheerleading squad—had gone on the bus with the football team to their travel game. As much as I try to be optimistic, it's hard to be left out. Everyone is gone.

I rest my elbow on the table and plop my chin in my palm to sulk. This is going to be a long football season if I must sit out the entire time. Dad goes behind the counter to grab our pizza, leaving me to stare out the window. The weather even matches my mood, overcast, with thick clouds threatening rain. With the temperature hovering right around that thirty-three-degree mark, rain will easily turn into freezing rain, creating the worst-case scenario for travel. I really hope the bus makes it back tonight, or I might be spending the whole weekend without my friends. I sigh heavily as everyone is experiencing junior year without me.

"I'm glad we have this time together," Dad starts when he returns with a small pizza, taking a moment to center it in the middle of the table, and we both dish up a piece of my favorite pepperoni and jalapeño. While dad stuffs the end of his napkin into his shirt collar, he adds, "I was hoping we could talk."

My expression may have been a bit guarded. Dad and I have always been close, but with everything going way wrong this year, I'm scared of what's next. "Talk about what?"

"What's up with Rocco?" Dad's dark eyes soften, but he doesn't hold back from taking a bite of his slice before he speaks again, "The coach called me and said he's been having a lot of issues with his temper, even more than usual."

"I don't know." I pick at the cheese strand that never ends as I try to politely nibble it off my slice. "You know how he is. He has a chip on his shoulder, and he doesn't let anyone talk to him."

"I know." Dad lowers his lashes, hooding his eyes, being hard on himself. The truth is, Dad has done about everything he can think of to help both Rocco and me succeed in life, but he's only one person. It was certainly easier when Mom was around, but she passed unexpectedly last year after a very short battle with breast cancer, and Rocco has had anger issues ever since. "I sure wish he'd talk to me."

"Maybe someday he will." I dab the corner of my mouth, ignoring the knot in my stomach that always buds when we talk about any of the changes our family has gone through this last year. I change the subject, "Hey, I have a question for you."

"What's that?" One of his bushy brows spikes over the other.

"Something happened to Rosie, my axolotl. I had her when I fell asleep last night, but when I woke up, she was missing. I looked all over for her, but with my knee throbbing to its own tune, I had to give up. Have you seen her?"

"I have not." Dad tilts his head, thoughtfully. "Not aside from the fact that every time I've seen you this week, you've had her on your lap."

"Right," I exclaim, as I love her so much. "I never let her out of my sight, and now she's gone."

"I'm sure she'll show up." Dad pats his hand on top of mine, just as a crowd of teens walk up outside the window.

It takes a moment for me to recognize the Bulldog blue, red and white. "Oh, look at that. The team must be home early. It looks as if they are all headed to the coffee shop."

I recognize my whole cheer squad and several of the players. My heart skips a beat when North passes in front of the window, with Rocco behind him. The crowd rushes across the street, and I feel a pang of envy as they all file into the coffee shop. *Just another thing I'm missing out on.*

"You should go." Dad coaxes softly. "I'll help you across the street."

Pulling one side of my mouth up into a lazy smile, I hate to leave him, but he understands. "Do you think I'll be crashing?"

"Not at all. You may not be able to cheer anymore, but you can sit at the coffee shop to hang out. You need to at least be able to do that much." Dad jumps to his feet and holds his hand out to help me up. "Besides, then you can keep an eye on that brother of yours."

"Thanks Dad." I take his hand, and limp forward, favoring my swollen knee as a bubble of excitement fills my chest. Finally, after a solid week of being left out, there's something I can do, too.

Six

Due to the forecasted sleet, our game got called after the third quarter, giving the win to us, and we make it home before eight. We're all hyped up, and head to our favorite spot, the old coffee shop by the school, for a celebration. It's nothing fancy, and the old guy who works here gives us a side eye more than a smile, but it's big enough we can all go, and it fits a teenager's budget.

Although, one thing about me is, I despise coffee. I love the smell, especially if it's freshly roasted, but I will gag on even the lightest coffee flavor. Blah, no thank you!

I order my chai tea, and head to the back booth, sliding in next to Rocco, who's trying to flirt with one of the cheerleaders. I forget her name, or maybe I never knew it, but she's the red-headed girl who's always next to Gia on the bottom of the pyramid.

"I think we lucked out tonight getting the game called," I say, trying to get in on the conversation.

"We wouldn't have to rely on luck if you could catch the ball." Rocco teases a smug smirk with both corners of his mouth. Sometimes, he doesn't know when to shut up. I had dropped two passes this game, and I admit I can play better, but it's not like it's on purpose. Swallowing, I bite back a rebuttal as every day it gets harder to be on a team with Rocco. I know he's been through a lot this last year, losing his mom, but that didn't slow him down on the football field, or with the ladies. If anything, he's gotten more popular, and it often seems like my presence is annoying to him, and he uses me as a verbal punching bag to inflate his own ego. Don't get me started on the weird threats to stay away from Gia. As if I'm some predator. I've known them both for over a decade.

I don't care to sit here with Rocco and be insulted. My gaze slides back to the counter, and I see my drink waiting for me. I slide out of the booth and stroll back through the narrow row of tables. Out of the corner of my eye, I recognize Gia standing next to her dad, both waiting at the counter as well. I quickly scan her body and let out a giant sigh of relief that she's standing. Engrossed in conversation, neither one of them notices me.

I slip my tea off the counter, raising it up and pause for a quick temperature check against my lip. It's perfect—not too hot or too cold—the Goldilocks of temps, and I take a giant sip before my taste buds register the bitter afternotes and a tornado of a dry heave spirals up from the bottom of my gut. I gag so hard, all while trying to avoid vomiting. "Blah," I choke out. "This is *super strong* espresso."

"Oh no!" Gia's gaze perks back at me as she registers what's happening. "You must have gotten mine. It was called, but I was letting it set for a while to cool."

It's too late, the espresso is making me feel ill, and I grab my stomach and gag again. "That has to be the most disgusting thing I ever drank."

"I'm so sorry." She reaches out, placing her hand on my back, giving it a sort of motherly pat, but the chemicals her touch ignite in my body sends a whirlwind of sparks to rapid fire in my heart. Add that to my near-vomiting and I'm about to lose my balance.

"Here's some water." Mr. Bella presents a glass, and I eagerly accept it, swallowing all of it while closing my eyes. The water cools my gut and resets my tase buds.

"You guys got back early tonight?" Gia's look of concern is still pinned between her brows. She's so unbelievably beautiful, but my gaze drifts to the back booth, and sure enough Rocco's glaring at me with narrowed eyes. He's never going to let up about this. I can't even have a simple conversation with Gia without him hovering.

"The game got called due to the weather forecast," I say with a concise grin as I slip my foot back away from her. "Let me pay for a new drink for you since I ruined yours."

"Don't mention it," Mr. Bella cuts in. "I took care of it."

The barista places another cup on the counter calling out, "Spiced chai."

"That's me." I nervously chuckle, as I feel so torn. I want so badly to talk to Gia, but also don't want Rocco to slam me against the wall again. Choosing the latter of the two options, I flash my palm up in a wave, and turn away from Gia, dragging my feet back to the booth.

Some days I can't wait to get out of this town. Not to put any distance between Gia and me, but you know when you've outgrown some people, and maybe even a place. That's clearly Rocco and me. Eight more months until graduation, and it can't come fast enough.

SEVEN

North

About a decade later . . .

Finally, it's the NFL season kickoff. I've been waiting for months, excited to try out my new, mounted 72-inch flatscreen. Of course, I've been using it for months, watching animal and nature documentaries, but that's not nearly the same as football. On my back porch, I've got Cajun seasoned chicken wings perfecting in my wood chip meat smoker. They'll be done by halftime.

Sunday excellence.

I ease down onto my soft leather La-Z-Boy recliner, kick up the footrest, and crack open a frosty Dr. Pepper. The carbonation bubbles burst out and fizzle against my palm. I'm almost salivating as I slowly raise the can to my mouth.

"Heeeeeelp!"

One of my brows hikes as I follow the sound, and I sit up straight, arching my neck to see out the window. Nothing out of the ordinary. Mr. Bella's old red Ford is running in his driveaway, but he's nowhere around. Maybe that's a little odd, but I'm sure he ran back in the house to get something.

It's not worth missing the first kickoff for.

"Heeelp me, please!"

I advance toward the door, bracing it open, but still, I see nothing. I scratch the back of my head as my gaze draws back to the TV. I missed the first kickoff. I glance at the clock counting down the minutes until the end of the first quarter. There is nothing I want to do more today than watch my Giants win, but I can't ignore someone screaming for help. I sigh, tucking my phone into my pocket as I rush out the front door.

My concern growing with each passing second, I follow the bellowing around the back of Mr. Bella's house to the detached double garage off the back alley. The overhead door is open, but I can't see inside of it. Stacks of boxes—every size and shape—overflow out the front. It's like it's moving day, or something. "Mr. Bella," I holler. "Are you there?"

"North?" His voice staggers from somewhere deep inside the caves of boxes.

"Yeah, it's me. You okay?" I inch closer, but there's no path to go between the boxes. "Where are you? What's all the hollering about?"

"Don't laugh," his voice is stern, echoing off the unfinished walls and cement slab floor. "I seem to have gotten trapped back here when I stepped on some of my fly trap paper, lost my balance, and knocked over a stack of boxes on top of myself."

My gaze scans the boxes, and again, I'm amazed how he got past the first row. I'm going to need a crane to get him out. "Um, hold on a second!" I pull out my phone, still assessing the stacks of boxes. If they are heavy, it could take an hour, or more, to get back to him. I couldn't help but feel an intense pang of regret. *I'm going to miss the game.* But deep down, I understand Mr. Bella needs me. "I'm calling for backup. We'll get you out."

I scroll through my contacts, looking for a number to call. I sure don't want to call Rocco. Even though he lives in town, he turned into one of those dudes I never care to see again. I scroll through my small list of names, landing on my group list for the football team I coach. They'd muscle these boxes out of here in a hurry, but if he's hurt, his family needs to know. Since I already established I'm not calling Rocco, that leaves me with *Gia.*

A ping sparks in my gut at the sight of her name in my phone. Gia and I hadn't spoken to each other since high school. I had all my dreams come true, getting drafted to the NFL right after high school. Actually, Rocco and I both got drafted, and it was such an exciting thing for our school and town.

My dream was short lived when I blew out my ACL during training, before I even played in a game. I returned home to attend college for coaching. It was around that time, I quickly discovered Rocco was illegally betting and cheating, and he got kicked out of the NFL. I was not the one to turn him in, but since I was the only person he knew that fully understood his secret, he blamed me for getting caught. I tried to tell him so many ways, it wasn't me who turned him in, but he always seemed to blame it on me.

After that, we drifted apart, as my life was heading in a different direction. I got a job teaching and coaching at my old high school. The housing crunch was in full steam, and I couldn't find a place to live. When my parents decided to retire, move to Mexico, and sell their house, I jumped at the chance to buy them out. Their house is in my district, and close to work. It was an afterthought when I remembered that Rocco and Gia's dad still lived next door.

Rocco hardly came home, so that isn't an issue. Gia moved further west, to the Hamptons, working in some fancy resort. When she does come home, I avoid going outside, or I stay late at work. We never had a falling out.

It's the opposite.

Gia and I never had much of anything, thanks to Rocco making sure I never got near her. Staying away didn't do anything to cure my affection for her, because even after all these years, the sound of her name makes my heart slam against my ribcage, reminding me of all the risks I didn't take in life. Not to mention, all the ways Rocco bullied me, and larger than anything else—all the love I've stored for Gia.

I rake my hand through my hair and cringe.

I can't believe I never asked her out.

I almost did, once.

I chickened out, instead asking her to save me one dance.

Ha! Not sure what I was going to do with one dance, but the thought of holding her in my arms for even a few minutes made my heart quake at a magnitude 9.0.

Later that night when I visited her, I tried to ask her out again. There was a moment where she looked at me as if she could think of me as more than a friend. My mouth went dry, and I couldn't get the words out fast enough before Mr. Bella showed up.

I take a deep breath, my memories telling too much truth. Rocco threatened to destroy me if I ever touched her. At first, I thought he was joking, but his pupils got all dilated, and he never dropped it.

I tried to pretend that I didn't love her.

I'd look the other way when we'd cross paths in the hall at school.

My feelings just continued to grow.

It was as if Rocco could smell them, because he was always there, too. He refused to get out of my way, and now after so many years have passed, I've still never had the chance to tell her how I feel.

"Hey, are you still there?" Mr. Bella hollers back through the boxes, inserting himself into my memories.

"Yeah." I blink, and remember he's still trapped. "Give me one moment, I'm calling Gia."

I swallow, coating my throat as this is going to take every ounce of strength I have.

EIGHT

Gia

As the sous chef of the resort's five-star restaurant, I take my desserts very seriously. I had my perfect round cakes cooling in the pans, and I'm starting work on my famous chocolate ganache to coat the layers. I drop the vat of butter in the pan and turn on the stove, taking a moment to adjust the temperature just right.

"Wow, Gia!" Grace exclaims as she returns to the kitchen with a matte black folder in her hands. Even with her blonde ponytail tussled under her hairnet, and one single wispy strand of hair dangling next to her face, she still looks like a model. "Someone is blackmailing you. They dropped off all these photos, and there's no note." She yanks a glossy 8 by 10 out of the packet, flashing it at me. "It's scathing."

Churning my stomach into knots, I advance towards her while frantically wiping my fingers on my apron. "Give me those." I tug the packet out of her hands, but my stomach loop easily relaxes. "These aren't embarrassing photos. These are my new headshots. I paid a lot of money to have them done." I flip through the pile of 8 by 10s. Sure, my glasses are bigger than average, and I've sprouted more than a freckle or two since moving near the beach, but there's nothing *scathing* about these.

She perks a feather brow at me. "Headshots?"

Half embarrassed, I lower my gaze. "I'm thinking of going on this new dating app called, *Your Last First Date.* My dad got a free match card the other day while he was standing outside his shop. He clearly isn't going to use it, so he gave it to me. I looked it up, and it has really good reviews, and frankly, I must be doing something wrong." I shake, the hopelessness of being forever single seeping in. "I'm not having any luck with the available dating pool."

"What?" Grace's perfectly pink-stained lips part into a gasp. "When were you going to tell me this secret?"

"It's not a secret." I drop my voice, remembering we're still at work. "I didn't think I needed to advertise it everywhere."

"I totally understand." She asserts with a giant supportive nod, and whispers, "Did your date last weekend not go well?"

"There wasn't anything *wrong* with him, but there wasn't anything right either," I continue in a hushed voice, hoping our manager, Marcie, doesn't overhear my personal life saga. "He was so distracted by everything. If he wasn't looking at his phone, he was ogling the table of women next to us. It's my pattern that I get men who don't care to spend quality time with me."

"I had no idea you were feeling so overwhelmed you were looking online." Grace's lips grow into a full smile. "Online dating is going to be so much fun. What else do you have up your sleeve?"

A chuckle falls from my lips. "Well, this morning it was a sock left over from the dryer." Before I can crack another joke about my lackluster life, my phone vibrates in my pocket. I pull it out, and my breath hitches in my throat.

North Newson.

His name sears a trail right to my heart. I hadn't spoken to him in years. Not that I ever forgot about him. He seems to be that one "what if" in my life that never resolved itself. If I'm honest, he's one of the main reasons I don't care to go home much. It's torture to my heart to see him over the fence. I'm instantly transported back to high school when I was head over heels for him.

Or maybe I'm not remembering the past feelings as much as I'm unable to push down current ones.

Either way, it's immobilizing.

"I'm going to step out back and take this," my voice floats out, while my eyes hang onto North's name.

"Oh, more secret dates." Her voice drops into a sweet giggle.

I wave her off as I step out the kitchen backdoor and into the private loading dock. The phone's ringing, and I dig deep and suck back a chestful of fresh air before I press the phone to my ear. "North Newson. What a surprise."

"Gia Bella. Your voice sounds exactly the same."

"I would hope so. Last I checked, I'm still me."

Expecting him to chuckle at my witty banter, his silence tips me off that this call is serious. I clear my throat. "How have you been?"

"I'm well, but that's not why I'm calling. I'm calling about your father."

Ice frosts my veins, stilling me. "Is he okay?"

"Oh, yeah," He rushes in a calming tone that soothes my nerves. "He's fine. Not in any trouble at all. Except, he's stuck in his garage."

"Oh." I nod even though no one is here to see me. This news isn't anything shocking, as my dad's hoarding situation has slowly gotten out of hand. I joked it would only be a matter of time before his stuff would swallow him up. "How bad is it?"

"His garage is a sea of boxes. I can hear him bellowing back there, but can't see him. I'm going to call some of my football players to help, or it will take me all night."

"I'm a couple hours away at work." I let out a sigh as I add the hours on the clock. "It'll take me a while to get there, but let me make some calls. I'll get a hold of someone who can help you. I'm so sorry he's bothering you."

"Oh, he's no bother. No need to send more help. I have it under control. I just felt like his family should know."

"Well, thank you. I appreciate it." Blinking my eyes, I push back the smallest tear as his thoughtfulness is so touching. North always was the most kind-hearted man. "I, ah, I'll figure something out with work and get back to you."

"No problem. I'll be busy digging him out."

His voice ticks up at the end as he is ready to sign off, but in a freak moment of bravery I cut him off. "It's great to hear your voice again." He immediately hushes, and the silence drags on for the longest beat before I tack on, "Anyway."

"Same," he softly quips.

A moment later and the line goes dead, and I'm running my hand through my needing-some-fresh-highlights hair.

Who am I going to call?

It's Friday night. Not that it would matter if it was Monday morning, I still wouldn't have more friends. I'm sure not calling Rocco. We'd had a falling out last year after his NFL career imploded amidst a cheating scandal, and he cut me out of his life.

North said not to bother sending help, but this is my dad. Someone needs to talk to him about the bigger issue. He got lucky this time, but what happens when he gets hurt? I can't put this off any longer.

I turn back toward the hotel, knowing I don't have anyone to call. This was a me problem. "Grace!" I call out, as I tiptoe back inside, ready to bargain with my future first born child. "Can you cover for me? I need to leave."

"Dad!" I call into the open overhead garage door, peering through the narrow pass in between the stacked-to-the-ceiling boxes. An echo ricochets back, but no answer from him. He's only lived here a couple of decades, but his garage is so jam-packed, it looks as if he's lived here a hundred years. Being a collector of all things, he hates to toss anything out if they might be useful. His thriftiness has gotten out of hand. My brows pin together as I turn back toward the house and continue up the broken steppingstones leading to the side door.

I forgo a traditional knock and open the side door. It creaks with the exact same squeal it did when I lived here. It's not that Dad is lazy, because he's not. He still works nearly every day at the pizzeria, but it's becoming clearer he's in some sort of funk, letting things go. "Dad!" I call out, "you alive in here?"

"Umph." His old man sigh wafts from the living room and I pad forward to find him sitting on his favorite recliner, watching ESPN, with an open jar of honey roasted peanuts on his lap. "You didn't have to come over," he grumbles.

"Yes, I did. I was worried. Are you okay?" Scanning his physique for any signs of physical damage, I find nothing out of place except for his unibrow pinned together in a lowered position, hinting at a bruised ego.

"It was nothing. I slipped on my vintage fly paper. I think it is defective because it really didn't need to be so sticky. You should have seen it, stuck on me like cement and tangled me up until I knocked over some boxes, and they trapped me."

Resisting the urge to roll my eyes at his lack of accountability, I instead scan the lone box in the corner of the room. "Did you get a recent delivery?"

Dad's gaze follows mine to the box. "Oh, that." He shakes his head, tacking on, "That's some of your brother's old high school football trophies. After he got kicked off the team, he wanted to throw them out. I'm saving them in case he ever wants to look at them some day."

I roll my bottom lip in and survey the rest of the house. Except for the box of stuff, it's actually pretty neat. There are no dishes in the sink, and his throw blankets are neatly folded. *Maybe the hoarding is not really that bad if everything is in the garage.* I mean, he can always close the door and not look at all his junk. "Well." I tsk, and stride toward the box, scooping it up. "Do you think we should tuck it away in Rocco's old room, so we don't have to look at it?" I'm already walking down the hall to Rocco's door. Dad's reply muffles as I turn the knob and immediately startle, taking a giant step back.

A mountain of stuff is about to crash into me!

"Aaggh!" I scream, and slam the door shut, ducking against it as crashing noises sound like a fireworks finale. *Who was I kidding?* It isn't just in the garage. I'm pretty sure every room, drawer, nook and cranny is stuffed, and dangerous! My eyes grow wide as I frantically search for my dad. "Dad, this is serious. You need help cleaning your house out."

"Nah, it's not an issue." He waves his hand dismissively. "It doesn't bother me."

"Dad, you almost died today because you have an insurmountable amount of clutter. It's a life-threatening issue. We're cleaning this out, starting now, with this room." I press my ear against the closed door, all the crashing noises have died off.

It should be fine. I swallow, and twist the knob slowly, pushing the door open.

Piles!

The stacks are not even neat like in the garage. There are mounds of clothes, and most don't even look worn. On Rocco's old desk, there're stacks of opened bills that I assume are paid, and for no reason I can think of—other than Dad hates to throw things away—they've been allowed to accumulate. There are boxes of old Christmas decorations I don't remember ever seeing in the house, and so many collections! He must have a collection of everything! Old books, model cars, footballs with every team logo on them, and so much sports memorabilia he could start a museum.

I inhale a deep breath and slowly let it out. "I'm going to need some coffee for this."

It's Saturday night, and I spent all day cleaning out Rocco's old room. Dad and I only had one minor argument about a stack of 1970's newspapers. Dad insisted we needed to save them. I offered to clip out the articles he wanted to save and make him a scrapbook, but he couldn't tell me which articles were even in there. At that point, I girl bossed those papers into the recycling. You'd think that would be the end of that, but no. Later when I was using the restroom and went on a hunt for some toilet paper, I found the newspapers had somehow escaped from the recycling bin and stuffed themselves underneath the bathroom sink. I can't fathom what's so special about them.

We ended up bargaining. He keeps the papers, and I get one single box with some of Rocco's football memorabilia: trophies, medals, photos, even old jerseys. It seems like everything football he'd ever owned from the time he was a little kid is in his old room, and I promised that I wasn't going to throw it away.

I wanted to. I certainly had to chew the inside of my cheek, to get through that conversation. I might have fibbed that first time I sternly said I wasn't throwing it out, but then there was a tiny tear in the corner of his eye, and I had to come up with a better plan.

He suggested donating the junk to the high school where Rocco played. Rocco is still a local legend. They will surely love to put this stuff in their glass display cases in the hall. Or at least that's what I need dad to think they are doing with it. It's just too painful in so many ways for us to keep this stuff around. Besides the fact that Rocco created one of the biggest NFL scandals and cut out his entire family, there isn't any room for it.

As I drive over to the school, my mind races with all the signs I overlooked about this hoarding issue. Clearly, I looked the other way when I shouldn't have, but I'm doing my best to right the situation now.

I smile nostalgically as I see the school. Some things never change. A sigh falls from my lips as Dad's old Ford putters forward over the rocky-road parking lot. Even after all these years, there's still the giant pothole near the entrance, and thankfully, I remember to slow for it. There must be something going on tonight as I can hardly find a parking spot. I jump out of the truck and grab the box. It would be better if I waited until Monday to call the principal and drop by, but I have to work next week. Surely there are some teachers here I can talk to, and they can pass my stuff to the right person.

I tuck my face down to keep warm and out of the chilly fall breeze. I should have grabbed a thicker jacket, as I had dressed to clean in old knee-ripped jeans and a faded sweatshirt, not considering I'd be making deliveries. Racing to the entrance, I'm easily able to enter the unlocked door.

I scan the lobby. It had been almost ten years since I was here, but boy am I instantly transported back, feeling as if it is my first day of school. The same blue carpet and white lockers. A ticket table is set up near the auditorium entrance next to a sign that announces a band concert. Even the not-quite-desirable smell is still the same. Like old buildings mixed with teenage drama.

I never thought much about high school after I left. I wasn't one of those kids who pined for those years. I had fun. I did the things and attended the events, but I was glad to move on. I slow my steps as I near the office. The lights are off, but this is the hall where all the cheerleading memorabilia is hung, and I have to see my old photo.

All the varsity squads for the last twenty years have a 5 by 7 framed photo. I quickly find my squad, cringing when I see my bangs. At the time, I remember quite clearly my plan was to hide my giant forehead, but this photo is evidence of the fact that it did quite the opposite. I turn on my heel, as my cheeks burn, and I'm glad I'm alone. Down the hall, the band door is open. I heard everything in their room is updated, and they finally got some fancy tiered seating. I stroll down the hall, curious to peek inside.

"Ahem!" A stern, deep phlegmy throat clears from behind me, startling me to stand up straight and pivot toward it. A stout man wearing a dark button-down shirt with a badge on it glares at me with lowered eyebrows. "Excuse me, ma'am. What are you doing here?"

I eye his badge, concluding he must be some sort of rental cop for the concert. "Sorry." I pull up one side of my lips into a half smile. "I don't have my hall pass."

Rent-a-cop has no sense of humor and doesn't even twitch a lip. "I'm going to have to ask you to come with me."

"Now, is that any way to ask a girl out on a date?" I'm not trying to be annoying, but this guy is too serious about his rented badge. I'm clearly not doing anything wrong. I'm standing in the hallway with a box of antiques.

"I see you have confiscated school jerseys in that box." Shortie rises to his toes, peering down into the box.

"I didn't steal this!" My jaw dramatically flops open. "I brought it here to donate. These are my brother's, Rocco Bella's, jerseys." As much as I didn't care to talk to Rocco anymore, it felt good to name drop him because he is famous. "He played quarterback here and holds all the school records—"

"Ma'am, I'm going to ask you one more time to come with me, or I will be calling the cops—"

"Gia! There you are." A familiar voice wafts from behind me as an adjacent classroom door sweeps open. As I pivot, the voice carries on, "Glen, she's fine. You can let her go. I asked her to come visit and bring that stuff."

I know that voice!

My heart thumps against my ribcage as I raise my gaze. North Newson.

He hasn't aged at all, with his dark-chocolate-espresso-brown eyes, still as dreamy as ever, in addition to his full mop of hair that falls to frame his eyes, drawing all the more attention to them. He looks better than a walking deep fried donut, and he's coming this way.

Nine

North

"Gia," my voice hangs on to every letter in her name, and it feels so right. I had heard Glen harassing someone in the hallway, the voice teasing familiarity, but when I heard her say her brother was Rocco Bella, my heart puttered to a screeching halt, and I knew I had to rescue her from creepy Glen.

I step into the hall, making up a story as I speak, "Sorry if you got lost. I should have given you better directions." I look back at Glen, my irritation with him growing with each passing second. "She's my guest. You can leave us alone now. I'll make sure she's properly escorted out when she's ready to leave."

Glen stutters out tsks, like an old engine that won't turn over but can't quite form a word. Obviously, his ego got deflated, and he takes a minute to regain his composure before he finally hmphs and heads out.

Gia places a perfect hand over her mouth, suppressing airy giggles. Not wanting to risk Glen circling back to find us laughing at him, I wave her inside my classroom. "Come on in here." She flashes me a sweet smile, sending a shiver down my spine. I couldn't help but follow her every step with my eyes, captivated by her graceful movements as she disappeared inside. I might have let out a giant sigh of relief that she didn't have a permanent limp. I dart inside right behind her, and we burst out laughing once the door closes.

"Thanks for saving me from whoever that was." She dramatically stares in the direction Glen went.

"It's Glen. He does the nightshift and gets a little carried away. I'm sorry you had to deal with that." My smile lingers, but I pause and remind myself to breathe. Even though I had just spoken to her the other day, it's the first time I've seen her in years, and she's stunning. A rush of excitement and nervousness spirals together. Her intense eyes lock onto mine. With the chalkboard as her backdrop, I can't help but feel like I'm sixteen again, staring at her. "I, ah, saw your car in your dad's driveway. How's he doing?"

"He's good." A single lock of dark hair falls in front of her shoulder as she thoughtfully shakes her head. "And thank you for rescuing him. I'm sorry I didn't make it back in time to help you. I had no idea things had gotten that bad, but I'm cleaning stuff out today. That's actually why I'm here." She peers down at the cardboard box she's holding. "I'm trying to donate some of Rocco's football trophies. I don't care to ever see them again, but I promised Dad I wouldn't throw them out. I know Rocco and you had a falling out, but he does still hold the school records. I thought the kids might want to see them. Do you think there's room somewhere for them?"

A deep heartburn sizzles in my chest, and I twitch at Rocco's name. Having lived in his shadow the entirety of my football career, I thought after I left the NFL, I'd finally break free from it.

That didn't happen.

Even now that I'm coaching a winning football team, I still get asked almost daily about Rocco.

I'm never going to get away from him.

But yet, this is *Gia* asking for a favor.

I'll do anything for her.

"Sure. You came to the right person." I tilt my head thoughtfully and reach forward. "I'm the head football coach now. I can put it up in the locker room."

Not that I really want to have to look at Rocco's dumb stuff, but if it makes her happy, I'm doing it.

A relieved sigh falls from her throat. "Thank you. I was getting nervous for a minute, thinking I might end up hauling it back to the house." A smile blooms on her lips, lighting up the whole room with her radiance, and reminding me how she always had that ability to spread joy just from the expression on her face. People just felt welcome around her. "One box down, at least a hundred to go."

Pulling my gaze from her smile, I force myself to walk the box over to my desk, pushing a mountain of still-needed-to-be-graded papers over. Doing my best to sound relaxed. I call back over my shoulder, "So, how long will you be in town?"

"Through tomorrow." She scratches at her earlobe, appearing a little extra fidgety than I remember her being. "I'll have to head back in the evening because I work Monday, but I'm hoping to be able to get through the garage before I leave."

I throw my head back, forcing a sarcastic laugh. "Good luck with that."

"Right." Her smile is still growing, which makes mine larger, too. It's been years since I've seen her, but this feels so different than previous times I've chatted with her. In the past, Rocco was always loitering near, with his nostrils flaring.

Rocco isn't here now.

This may be my only chance to spend some time with her.

I cocked my eyebrow. "Do you have time for me to show you something?"

"Ah, yeah." She nods, her eyes widening, becoming even more captivating. "Please do."

With my index finger, I point behind her where a fish tank lines the back wall, and it is home to one of the coolest creatures on the planet.

"You finally got a real axolotl?" She steps forward, all the features on her face are etched in anticipation. "It's exactly like the one you gave me but waaay smaller."

She remembers the gift.

My heart rockets into my ribcage.

Swiping my tongue over my bottom lip, I force my lips to keep moving. "I'm impressed you still remember what they're called. Most people have no idea they exist."

She's standing in front of the fish tank now; her button nose almost presses glass. "I wouldn't either if it weren't for you. That stuffed animal is one of my favorite gifts I've ever gotten."

I turn my head, doing my best to hide the heat on my cheeks.

"Oh, look how cute he is!" She gushes as she pushes her finger on the glass, and he swims right to her. "I can't believe he's in school."

"The kids love him too, and since I teach biology, the school actually gives me a little stipend for projects, so it was a no brainer."

"I love that you got one finally." She rotates back to me, and I wouldn't have believed it is possible with her previous smile already radiant, but now her whole face is beaming, emitting so much exuberance, it's hard not to think it's genuine. I'm vastly aware this is one of the few times I've been alone with her. Except for the stolen moments we used to have under the bleachers, and that night at her house, there aren't any other times I can think of. That night is a haunting reminder of the time I failed at asking her out. I still think about what might have happened if her dad hadn't barged in.

Shoot, that was years ago, and who knows when I'll see her next.

I might not ever get another chance to ask her out again.

My palms are awash with sweat. It really is now or never. We aren't going to be able to small talk for much longer. "Gia." I clear my throat, my heart fluttering with nerves and uncertainty. I've never wanted anything more than for her to say yes.

"What?"

"Ah. I know it's late, but I'm done here, and headed out. I'm, ah, wondering if you want to grab a coffee with me?"

Her eyes flick side to side before replanting on me. "You mean right now?"

"Yeah, if you don't have anything else going on, I'd love to catch up."

She doesn't pause for even a beat. "I'd love to."

I swallow a larger than average swallow. Okay, it's a gulp. It took me years to do this. An immediate surge of relief washes over me, until I realize asking her out is the easy part. That was one sentence. Now, I have to remain calm for the next hour.

My heart constricts, begging me not to blow this.

Ten

Gia

North and I stroll down a quaint street to the coffee shop that, to my surprise, has recently been bought out by a new franchise called The Coffee Loft. For an early Saturday evening, the shop is extremely bustling. We pass through the heavy door and are instantly met with the aroma of the deepest roasted coffee and cinnamon, making saliva swell in my mouth. "This place is adorable," I coo, taking in the new remodel and the rows of unique coffee cups hung on the wall, and finally latching my gaze on the chalkboard menu on the back wall.

With every possible flavor anyone could dream up, I have no idea how to pick just one. We shuffle our feet until we get to the front of the line, where we are greeted by a blonde woman with a ponytail pinned on the top of her head. "Chai guy, how are you?"

"Good evening, Portia, I'm good." He slowly pulls out his wallet while keeping his attention forward, "And you."

"I'm still brewing." They both laugh at the pun, and I smile, already feeling welcome.

North extends a hand toward me. "You can go ahead and order."

Without having had much of a chance to read the rather extensive menu, I eeny-meeny-moe the fall flavors in my head until I land on the last one. "Ah, I'll try the frosted maple latte."

"Great choice." The barista, who I now know is named Portia, punches some digits into her tablet and shifts her gaze to North. "And your usual spiced chai?"

"Yes, ma'am." He taps his debit card to the scanner before I have a chance to offer to pay.

"You guys can grab a seat, and I'll bring them right out." Portia grins at us before she turns her back to pour our milk.

"She has a nickname for you." I turn and whisper under my breath. "You must come here often."

"Yeah, it's the closest place to the school." We shimmy down the narrow aisle of tables until we get to the only open booth in the back. We both slide in, and North continues the conversation, "They're swamped in the mornings, and I usually don't have time to wait. Somehow, I made this a daily habit on my way home from work. Portia is one of the owners, and she's always so nice."

"And you are addicted to the spiced chai?"

"Addicted makes it sound so negative. Let's just say I have a high chai absorption rate, and I'm not much of a coffee drinker. I love the smell but can't stand the taste."

"Don't like coffee. I'm not sure if we can be friends." I bite back a fit of laughter as I recall when I almost made him vomit so many years ago. "I remember when you grabbed my straight espresso by mistake."

"Yes," he quips, his cheeks growing pink. "That was the second time I tried it, and it was not successful. Ever since then I've stuck to the chai."

"What?" I tilt my head closer, pretending to have a hard time hearing. I couldn't help but notice the way North's eyes light up when I tease him, so I keep going. "That menu is packed with amazing flavors, and you haven't tried anything else?"

"That's sort of how I am." His easy smile falls into place, and it does everything to make me feel comfortable, while pulling me to him. He looks exactly how he used to, still the most handsome man I've ever seen. He tacks on, "If you haven't noticed, I like my routines."

"How would I know that?" I tease, as so many sparks of connection fire between our gazes. It feels amazing to banter with North. "I haven't seen you in years."

"I guess we have Rocco's junk to thank for bringing us together again."

"I guess." My gaze falls to my lap, where I had started to pick at my fingernail. I still my hands and ask softly, "Do you talk to him much?"

"More than I'd like." He blows out a hard breath right as Portia arrives and quietly slides our drinks onto the edge of our table. We both take our cups, and I eagerly take a sip of mine, while he places a palm over the top of his lid. "At first, I didn't really believe he did all that bad stuff, and that's what made it hard for me to see his life fall apart."

"Same," I quip. "At first, I couldn't fathom he was that person, either."

"When he moved back to town and bought that car dealership, I was surprised because I had assumed he went broke paying for the lawyers. I tried to come around as a friend, but there were an awful lot of closed-door deals going on. Then out of nowhere he became the town mayor by that landslide write-in vote, and I was blown away. How can anyone with a criminal record be in his position? He must be paying everyone off, and I still don't have a clue where he gets his funding. I don't want anything to do with that."

North shifts his jaw side to side, as if he's grinding his teeth. "The kicker is that he is practically my boss because his dealership is the biggest sponsor to my football team. As much as I'd like never to see him again, a couple times a year I have to take a photo with him, or sit by him at some booster dinner."

"Yeah, I've seen his name in the paper a few times for his support of the football team." It doesn't sting to hear that North doesn't talk to Rocco anymore. I'd mostly gone numb to any news about Rocco. He was the golden child growing up, and that would have been enough of a shadow to live in, but when he made it to the NFL, his whole personality changed. "We don't have to talk about him anymore. I think we've both tried to move out of his shadow long enough."

"What would you like to talk about?" His lips curl up, higher on one side. "What have you been finding at your dad's?"

"Well, aside from the sports junk I found at the house, I also found a collection of bird houses. Say, you like biology. Do you think your students would maybe like twenty-seven bird houses? It could be a class project. Adopt a bird forest," I ramble, hoping I'm persuading him. "Extra credit if you get a bird to move in. Think of the options."

His laugh is instant. "Sure, I can take them off your hands if that makes you happy." My gaze locks with his. He's so dialed in to me right now, sitting across from me. Not at all like the last few dates I'd been on where the guy had been distracted.

Not that this is a date.

It's just coffee.

He takes a slow drink of his chai and lowers the cup back to the table. "Okay, so we have football trophies and bird houses. Anything else?"

"The better question is what didn't I find. He has a collection of everything from rocks and seashells to teapots and towels. It never ends."

"And he's fine with you giving away all his stuff?"

"No." I fight back a small tear as this is the first time I've been able to let out any stress over this predicament. Hearing my dad had been trapped by his stuff had been overwhelming, and I have so much guilt over not helping sooner. "He's not fine with it, but I'm doing it anyway. I booked a therapy appointment for him to try to get to the bigger issue, and he is so upset with me for doing that, but I have to put my foot down. I love him. I don't need to have a Lifeline Alert about him being swallowed up."

"It's okay, you had no idea it was that bad." His hand slides across the table, and he gently places his palm on mine. "You're doing a good job." He says it so convincingly I actually believe him. "If you want," he goes on, "I can stop over tomorrow and help take out a load. I mean, that is if your dad doesn't mind me helping."

"Dad doesn't mind you helping at all. He's always had a soft spot for you." *Not as big as the soft spot I have.* "We'd both love it if you can help."

"It's settled. I'll come over in the morning after Sunday service." He sneaks a look at his watch, the sparkle in his eyes dimming a little. "It's almost closing time. I hate to get kicked out." His words are slow and measured, like he's torn.

I flash a look at the clock on my phone. A half hour had gone by, but it felt like five minutes. "Oh, I didn't realize it was getting so late." I shimmy out of the booth. "I didn't mean to keep you so long. I truly was just dropping off a box, but I enjoyed your company."

"Don't apologize. The pleasure is all mine." He gives me a crooked smile. My toes curl as we stroll together toward the door, extending our goodbye way longer than it needs to be. "Thank you for the coffee."

"You're welcome. Thank you for having coffee," he replies.

I can't help but feel a sense of contentment wash over me. We follow the streetlamps back to the school. The lamps cast a warm glow on the sidewalks, and something about the moment feels a little magical. We walk side by side, but I catch myself staring at his strong arms, wondering what it would be like to link an arm into his. Before my cheeks warm, I let a sigh out, figuring it's best to wait for him to make his move. "Thank you for showing me the Coffee Loft. I'll have to try them again. Next time I think I'll try the cherry mocha." I stop in front of dad's truck, and turn toward him, enjoying how easy it is to be with him.

"I'm sure the next time I go, I'll have the spiced chai." A glimmer sparks from the corner of his eyes, and it almost melts me.

"Thanks for walking me back to my car." My gaze paces to the truck and then back to North. I don't want to get in the truck. Behind him, the streetlamp glows, setting the ambiance as the light wind tousles the tips of his hair, doing everything to make this moment feel romantic.

"You're welcome. It was easy since you parked next to mine." His eyes bounce off his car, and land back on mine. "Well, I'm leaving now. Tell your dad, hi."

"I will." I place one hand on my door, still not wanting to get in the truck, despite my cheeks starting to sting in the chilly air. North's standing so close, our breaths waft together as his gaze bounces around my face.

"Night." His feet are cemented, and he's not moving.

"See you tomorrow." I slide only one foot close to the truck, hoping he'll maybe try to kiss me, or shoot, ask me to hang out longer. It's really not that late for Saturday night.

"Yeah, I'll call before I come over."

"Sounds good." I slowly open my door, and I climb inside, my heart sinking a little. "Bye."

"Yeah. Nice seeing you again." His feet still don't move, and it's not my imagination that he's wanting to ask me something else, but it's just not working. It's beyond awkward now.

"Nice seeing you, too." I put my hand on my door, closing it a bit.

"Okay. Bye." He turns toward his car, and I quickly shut the door before we invent another fifteen ways to say goodbye. I never remember him being that uneasy before, but at least he wasn't as shy as he used to be.

He definitely is still thoughtful, and as good looking as ever. I turn the truck on and steer forward, seeing that North's in his car, politely waiting for me to pull out. He waves. I wave back. I move in front of him, and wave again. In the rear view mirror his reflection waves back at me.

Eleven

North

Somehow, I make it to bed, but now I'm lying here flat on my back, hands locked behind my head, staring at the ceiling. I don't settle as I replay everything I said to Gia over and over in my head. It is so easy to converse with her. She was so attuned, and acted like she had nothing better to do than spend time with me, though she has a literal mountain of work to get back to at her dad's house.

My eyes drift to my alarm clock. 2:14, and I'm still wide awake with a cheesy grin on my face. I can't help but wonder if things would have been different for us had I not been so shy. I had fallen in love with her literally the first time I saw her, but being shy, I made friends with Rocco first. I thought he could be the bridge to bring us together, but it had turned out to be the opposite. All he ever did was warn me to stay away from her. I tried for years to forget about her, but it was useless. There's always a gigantic pull when she is near, like my soul recognizes her presence, and I don't want to deny that anymore.

Even if I wanted to, I don't think I can. It's been escalating so much. Now that I've finally had a chance to sit down with her, I feel like if I don't let her know how I feel soon, I'm going to explode.

I get up early, head over to the church, where I sit in the same pew I've sat in every week for the last decade. After the service, I stop at the Coffee Loft for my daily spiced chai and that cherry mocha Gia had mused about. While I wait for our drinks, I tap my leg and stare at the menu. I should get something for Mr. Bella, too. I have no idea how he likes his coffee. Wanting it to be a surprise, I don't text to ask. "How about an extra mocha," I add to my order after Portia made my other two drinks.

"Absolutely, chai guy." She smiles at me coyly. "Are you seeing your lady friend again today?" The mere mention of Gia makes my heart stutter like a manual car that can't find its gear. "Who said she is my lady friend?"

"She's a lady, and I assumed she's a friend. Most people don't have coffee with their enemies." She holds on to a teasing smirk as she hands over a drink carrier with three cups.

I grab the drink carrier and simply say, "Thanks for the drinks."

"See you tomorrow." She waves at me until I turn my back. As I walk out the door, I text Gia.

Me: Are you ready for backup?

Gia: Yes! I found his stored canned food collection. Some of these pickles are older than me and have horns growing out of them!

The anticipation of seeing her sets my gut in fire knots. There've been so many times I've wanted to spend time with her that I can't believe it's finally happening. Though, I chuckle that it's not the romantic picnic or walk on the beach, I would have wished for. Nope. I'm literally going over there to clean out her dad's junk.

Yet, I couldn't be more excited, and I grin all the way to her house.

After parking in my driveway, I kill the engine, grab the drinks, and cross the front yard to her dad's. I've taken this path so many times under the pretense of seeing Rocco, when I was actually doing all I could to get a glimpse of Gia. Even after all these years, the grass never regrew fully. I make it to the front step. It's barely forty degrees out, but my palms gloss with sweat.

I'm sure it's the coffees.

It couldn't be anything else.

It's definitely not my stomach flutters.

I shuffle my feet a few times before I decide on the perfect stance to take. I need one that doesn't make me look too eager, yet excited to see her. I hold the drink carrier by the handle and knock quickly before casually leaning against the house with my free hand. All the effort to look relaxed is wasted when Mr. Bella promptly swings open the door.

"North, what a neighborly thing to do." He stands back, and I pass over the threshold. "Gia was telling me you're helping today." He leans in close, dropping his voice to a whisper, "Between you and me, I don't need any help. I'm allowing her to do this because I think she's miserable and misses—" Gia rounds the corner, and Mr. Bella interrupts himself mid-sentence shouting out, "It looks like you brought refreshments. What a saint!"

Gia's gaze catches mine, and a ping blasts to my heart. "Hey," she says softly, the sweetest smile curling on her lips. "I was half-expecting you to have a late awakening about what you agreed to do, and bail."

"No." Shaking my head, I struggle for the right words. Words to tell her there isn't anywhere else I'd rather be. I'm more than willing to throw out moldy food if it means I can see her. "I'm a man of my word. I'm here as I said I would be." I retrieve her drink from the carrier and offer it to her. "And, I picked up the cherry mocha you wanted to try."

"That's very sweet of you." Her lashes lower to the cup, and she doesn't wait to sip out of it. "Thank you."

I pivot and turn back to Mr. Bella. "I couldn't remember how you take your coffee, so I grabbed you one of Gia's mochas too. I hope that's acceptable."

"It's much appreciated." He takes the cup from my hand, and with his free hand pats my back the way he's always done. "Thanks, son."

"So." Gia's voice ticks up a notch, taking on an adventurous tone. "Shall I show you to the pantry and the mystery pickles? I don't have the stomach to dump them out myself. I'd love to stand back on that one."

"I got it." I step toward the kitchen, ready to banter. "My stomach's as strong as steel. If you've got petrified pickles, I can handle it."

Gia opens the large walk-in pantry and motions to the bottom shelf. There're rows of mason jars with dark murky water with barely visible shadows of items inside. "Have at it." Her shoulders bounce as if she's suppressing a dry heave. She's clearly in agony, but I find her animation quite adorable.

"I'll be across the kitchen, sorting through his shot glass collection."

"Hey!" Mr. Bella pipes up with his nose toward the cupboard. "You'd better not get rid of any of those. They're souvenirs from our travels."

"Dad, you don't even drink." She whips open the cupboard to display stacks of shot glasses, one from every state, and every sports logo ever.

"They might be worth money someday." Mr. Bella advances toward the cupboard, but Gia maintains her position, blocking him from getting nearer.

"They'll be worth money now, because I'm selling them on eBay." She's stern in her stance, revealing how feisty she is, and it makes my heart pitter even faster. I don't think there's anything about Gia I don't admire. Even though she can be a little sassy, it's not in a loose cannon kind of way. She always retains her softness. She just has that ability to make the people around her fold.

He rocks back on his heels, glaring at her. "Now I didn't say you can do that."

"*Dad*," She says his name so gently, it's as if she's talking to a baby bird. "If you let me clean these out, I promise I won't touch your hat collection."

He sucks in a hard breath before quickly spitting out, "Deal."

I try not to show my immediate glee as Gia and I share a victory eye lock. It's random, but yet so normal, it throws my heart into a whirlwind spin. One side of her lips curls up. If there is ever a smile to set off sparks, it's hers.

"This needs to be the last box." Gia covers her yawn with a flattened palm as I skim another giant box off the stack of doom in the back of the garage. We've cleaned all day, and now we're burning the midnight oil under the single 60-watt bulb light fixture. It sounds like drudgery but it's not. We've been laughing like kids, talking about the lost years, and sharing stolen smiles as if we're teenagers. My heart is fluttering so hard, it feels like it's in spring training camp. "I can't believe I kept you this long," Gia speaks through another yawn, this one making her eyes water.

"I'm not a prisoner. I want to be here." Each time I smile at her, we hold our gazes a little longer. At first, I thought it may be wishful thinking. She's being nice to me because I'm helping her with this never-ending junk pile. As the looks got longer, smiles turned flirtier, and I can't deny the chemistry at this point. "But I'll agree. Last box, and then we call it a night. We both work in the morning, and you still need to drive home."

"What do you think it is?" Rubbing her hands together in front of the box, she builds anticipation before digging in. "Another bug collection?"

"Judging from how heavy this one is, I'm going with more tools." I lean over and flip open the box flaps one by one.

"I hope it's not another box of clothes. That last one had way too many clothing moths in it for my comfort."

"Nah, it's too heavy to be clothes." I peer inside until I make out stacks of flat, black, and vinyl. "Records!" I gleefully report.

"Another box of records." She scoots closer, and we both take turns pulling them out to read off the funny names, "*Yummy, Yummy, Yummy.*"

"That sounds yummy," I tease.

"I actually remember playing this one when I was a kid." Her smile is so big, it shows all her perfectly even teeth. "Oh, The Everly Brothers," she coos and holds up the next one. "They were my mom's favorite when she was younger."

"1963." I read the date of release on the record. "It's crazy to think that wasn't that long ago, and look how music has changed. Everything is digital now."

"Sixty years." Her eyes widen as they snag on the next record still in the box. "*My Girl*! I wish we had a record player because I loooove this song."

"I'm sure if we keep digging, we'll find one or two." We both chuckle lightheartedly, but I sneak my phone out of my pocket, tap on the YouTube app, and type. "I might have something better than a record player."

Her eyes shift to me when I tap on the Temptations video, and the first few chords of the song ring through my phone. I set my phone on the box as her gaze goes to watch the video, but that's not what I have in mind. Instead, I hold out my hand, gesturing for her to stand. "I think I still owe you a dance."

"Are you for real?" Her brows raise, but she slips her hand into mine, and suddenly time slows way down.

"I hope I'm not too late." Of course I'm asking about the dance, but everything in my expression wants to make it about the possibility of *us.* My breath is even as soon as I wrap my other hand around her back and lead her into a twostep. Holding her is everything I dreamed it would be, and worth the wait times one thousand. The song is an interesting choice for a first dance as it's a bit of an up-tempo beat that causes us to sway together more than embrace tightly, and it's impossible not to sing the lyrics. We both drown out the singer through our off-key belting, but we are giggling nonstop by the time the song ends.

"It's been too much fun today, North." When the song is over, she sighs dreamily and slips out of my arms, heading back to the box of records, staring down at them. "Should we keep the records, or sell them?"

"Vinyl can be worth a lot of money, and you can't replace it easily. I'd say, this is one thing he can hold onto."

"Deal." She closes the box and pushes it back against the wall. "He can keep them." Standing up straight, she brushes off her jeans. "As promised, that is the last box. Thank you for helping."

"The pleasure is all mine. I really enjoyed spending time with you." Her smile lingers in what I have come to recognize as her flirting smile. "So, you are heading back home tonight. Are you going to return any time soon?"

"Oh yeah." She dramatically scans the rest of the boxes. "I haven't made a dent, and I'm not a quitter. I'll be back up next weekend."

"I look forward to it. Give me a holler, and I'll come help."

"I hate to bother you again. This is an awful lot of work, but I do look forward to seeing you again. Maybe we can do something else, too?"

"Yeah…I'd like that, too." I'm not a genius, she's fishing for me to ask her out, but something feels off. It's not for lack of flirting, but there's a knot in my gut, begging me to play it safe. "Ah, my boys actually have a game on Friday night. If you make it back early, you're more than welcome to come watch."

"A football game?" Her gaze angles away, as if floating back to her memories. "Boy, I don't think I've been to that field since you blew out my knee."

"You'll be safe." I hold both my hands up as if I'm under arrest. "I promise, I'll watch my big clown feet, and nothing bad will happen. You might have some fun."

"Maybe I'll make a point to get off work a little earlier so I can come."

"Yeah, I'd love to see you again."

"Me too." I zip my lips, vowing not to go into the longest goodbye again. This time I gaze into her eyes, enjoying how they seem to change colors as they sparkle under the faint garage light. Part of me craves to wrap my arms around her and pull her close. From the look she is giving me, I know she'd kiss me. We've known each other twenty years, it's not like it's too soon, but another part of me wants to savor the sweetness we have between us right now. I don't need to rush anything.

I pull the string on the garage light, and we walk together out of the open overhead door. We are quiet as we walk side by side to her door. I wait on the grass as she hops up the steps and I call to her, "Night, Gia."

"Night, North." She flashes a wave at me and her soft smile beams before she ducks inside.

Sighing, contentedly, I head across the yard to my house, humming the tune to *My Girl,* when something catches my eye. A box is sitting outside of the garage on the driveway. I don't remember putting it there. Maybe Gia dragged it out to make more room? It should be fine there until morning, but you never know...it might be something valuable. Just to be safe, I circle back, grab the box, and take it inside my house. I can run it over to Mr. Bella tomorrow when I see him outside.

Once inside, I place the box on the kitchen table. The top flaps aren't taped shut, looking as if we already went through this box. I don't remember it though. Curiosity piques, and I lift the corner of one flap. Bulldog red, blue and white meets my gaze, and a poster of our old high school football team comes into focus. Now that I know it's nothing personal, I flip open the flap and take the poster out. It's a game schedule with our old team roster.

Boy, Mr. Bella didn't get rid of anything.

Near the top of the photo, Rocco and I stand next to each other, arms around each other's shoulders, being the best friends we were back then. Shaking my head, I now know loyalty was only one way. I tried my hardest to be his best friend, even staying away from Gia after he asked me to, but that loyalty didn't get me anywhere. When news of his cheating scandal broke, I tried to give him the benefit of the doubt. He made up lies about his teammates to frame them. I defended him publicly, which almost ruined my career as a coach.

I wish I believed he'd learned his lesson, but I've noticed a pattern where he always gets what he wants. His life has taken him on such a different path, and he's known for hanging out with some of the shadiest business owners, and even politicians. I know one thing…he's not a man you want to cross.

A spiral of shivers trickles down my spine.

Rocco doesn't even talk to Gia anymore.

She said so herself.

Rocco can't possibly still be obsessed with keeping us apart. That was high school. Kid stuff. Gia's a grown woman now

Could he still care?

Twelve

Gia

"You sure are cleaning fast." Grace stands back as I shuffle my empty dessert pans through the dish area, blast spraying each one before pushing them into the automatic dishwasher. Normally, I wait for the hired dish boy to do this. However, he's been on his break for longer than usual, and I'm anxious to get on the road. "I have plans to go to a football game." Hot water steam fogs the little wispy hairs that frame my face, and I brush them to the side.

"I thought you swore off football after Rocco...you know." Grace is always the curious type, poking her nose into my business, but she does it in the most loving way, I can't even pause.

"Not NFL. High school. Actually, my old high school where I used to cheer. However, I'm going to watch the *coach*, not the players." I can't resist a lofty smile as I do one final inspection over the kitchen, not wanting to leave any messes. I've restored it to predinner status with gleaming countertops, and every pot and pan is hung neatly in its place. The only thing left to do now is pull meat from the back freezer for tomorrow, but Grace always insists on doing that on her own, since she's the head chef.

When I finally draw my focus back to her, her feathered brows waggle at me. "Oh, is that so?"

"I think it is so…" I chuckle airily, as this whole week I've been extremely giddy, lighthearted, and nothing can put me in a bad mood.

She smirks knowingly. "So that's the real reason you spent all weekend at home?"

"No." I shake my head, as the stacks of boxes still cloud my brain. "I went there to clean, but I reconnected with someone, and well, we are *connecting. "* My voice trails off into another giggle. "I'm excited to see him again. And, then tomorrow, I'll clean out all the junk."

She sighs, as if she's holding back hordes of advice, but heads back to her prep area, where pans of chicken breast are already prepped, but because she's a perfectionist, she grabs a ramekin of olive oil and a brush and dabs a little on each one. "What are you doing with all the purged junk?"

"Ah, it depends on what it is. If it's worth the money, I'll sell it online. If it's usable, but not worth any money, I'll donate it." The dish boy still isn't back, but I turn to

Grace anyway. "If it's okay, I'm going to head out early. All my brownies are cut, plated, and chilling. I even did all the dishes, which clearly isn't the job of a sous chef."

Her grin is instant, teasing yet supportive. "I'm going to need a full report on Monday, but have a great weekend."

"Thanks." My cheeks heat, as I head to the back door, and grab my coat off the hook. Despite being in a hurry, I still pause to peer at the ocean, my daily unwinding, and the sole reason I moved here. I'd dreamed my whole life of living near the ocean. With the meager wages of a cook, I never got close, but I get to work on beachfront property every day, which is close enough for me.

The sun is setting off a kaleidoscope of colors in the sky that reflects off the low tide. There's a soft wave teasing the shore, bringing in random strings of algae as sea treasure. I inhale the salty air and can't help but feel blessed. It's a tad interesting how I had been in a hurry to leave my hometown, but now I rush back home with butterflies in my gut. I'm left wondering if maybe my being in a huge hurry to move away made me miss out on something—or someone—better?

It's first and ten when I scramble through the already-filled bleachers to find a seat near the team. Friday night football is like a holiday in our town, and I quickly determine I'm going to the nosebleed seats. As I pivot to climb the stairs, a husky voice bellows out above the cheers of the crowd, "Gia! I saved you a spot."

A couple of women near me give me a sly smile, and suddenly I'm sixteen again with my first crush, all the butterflies spiral into my gut. I practically float down the steps. True to his word, North saved me one of the best spots, right behind the guys. Across the steps, the band toots out the school song, and it's all I can do not to make a cheerleader high V, as I practiced this song so much, I could dance to it in my sleep.

"I hope this is okay." North quickly leans in, putting a Nike on the bleacher below me. "I had to bribe a lady with a bucket of popcorn to give it up."

"It's perfect." The air is crisp, and stings to inhale. I pull my canary-yellow knit mittens out of my coat pocket and slip my hands into them.

"I'm glad you made it. I'll find you after the game." He strolls backwards onto the field, waving at me. One side of his lips is higher than the other, and a single dimple drops below it like a little exclamation point to his smile.

"Good luck!" I tug my beanie lower to cover the bottoms of my ears. It's been years since I sat outside on metal bleachers in the frigid air. I clearly forgot I should have brought something to sit on. My teeth chatter through each quarter, but there's no way I'm leaving because there's nothing I'd rather do than support North.

North has been amazing for the team—and the whole town knows it—bringing the Bulldogs to the state championship the last two years. It ignited a plethora of school spirit that has taken over the town. Every seat in the stadium is colored white, red, or blue, and flags and posters dot the rows of fans.

A tinge of sadness buds in my chest as I recall how the crowd used to cheer like this for Rocco when he was the town hero. I never assumed he'd always stay in the limelight, but I sure didn't expect him to become such a disgrace.

"Excuse me, ma'am." A young kid taps me on the shoulder, and I turn to find him holding a hot chocolate out. "This is for you."

"I'm sorry, I didn't order that." I tap my coat pocket, feeling for my wallet to pay because it sounds like the perfect thing to warm me up.

"It's yours, and it's paid for." He pushes it further toward me. "Coach Newson put it on his tab."

"Oh." My lips form a perfect O, as a ping spirals right to my heart, and I eagerly accept it. "Well, isn't that thoughtful." The hot chocolate is the secret sauce to keep my teeth from chattering, and I didn't realize how thirsty I was as I quickly finish it.

Before I know it, the guys line up for their final defensive play, and the ball is quickly intercepted. The crowd jumps to their feet, and everyone screams their hearts out while the ball is carried all the way to the endzone. It's a play for the movies as time runs out right when the winning touchdown is scored. I'm back in cheerleader mode, standing on the bleachers, screaming with everyone else. "Bulldog Victory!"

I pump my fist in the air, and the crowd around me cascades down the bleachers, rushing the field. I get caught up in the excitement and run right to North. His open-mouth grin displays all his joy as he effortlessly scoops me up, swinging me around, and we scream out in excitement all the while I'm acutely aware that *I'm in his arms.*

Like his strong masculine arms that have never looked better. Yep, those are the ones. They're wrapped all the way around me, and he's holding me right next to his chest.

Yep, that's strong and masculine, too, and I would have definitely remembered if I'd felt that before. The musky scent of his aftershave permeates off of him, and I'm being consumed by it in the best way.

This is better than winning the football game.

After twirling me for more than a few complete circles, North sets me down...but he doesn't let go, his eyes lock on mine. A bolt of electricity slams into my heart, completely disabling me. Being this close to him is all I ever wanted, and it's better than I could have imagined. He's tall, but so am I, and we fit together perfectly. As I tilt my head back just a little, I can see directly into his eyes, and they capture me, drawing me further into his joy. He drops his chin next to my ear, and whispers, "Meet me under the bleachers," before he pulls away, while motioning with his head toward the team huddle. "Wait for me."

My lips curl up, all the while my heart pounds against my rib cage, and I step back, waving until he runs to meet up with his team. His dark wavy hair ruffles under the congratulatory pats on the head. Seeing him so happy makes my heart swell with even more joy.

Taking the long way back to our little spot under the bleachers, I absorb the aroma of the field. Popcorn and fresh air—it all comes rushing back at once. All the nights I watched Rocco play, many years as a cheerleader. After he got kicked out of the NFL, I was embarrassed to show my face anywhere that had anything to do with football, not realizing I lost one of my passions too. I loved watching the games with dad. Even with all those memories of watching Rocco, I can't find one single memory where I wasn't also secretly watching North. He was always in my peripheral vision, but in the center of my heart.

"Hey!" North jogs my way, his voice hoarse from all the screaming. By now the wind is in full force, and light flurries are swirling, causing the tall trees behind the stadium to sway.

"That was fast," I call back to him, while rubbing my mittens together and shuffling my feet. As the sun had gone down below the horizon, it had gotten so much colder out.

"Yeah, it's just nasty out." He slides in beside me as if it's natural for him to reach a protective arm out, wrapping me in his warmth. "You're shaking."

"I'll be okay." I still under the warmth of his arm. "Great game."

His espresso eyes lock on me. "I couldn't be happier."

"I would say," I blurt out over my chattering teeth.

"Not about the game though." His eyes sparkle with so many hues of gold and copper, it's as if they are putting on a tiny fireworks show. "I couldn't be any happier because you are here."

My throat dries, and I swallow as my chatters are stopped with warmth pooling in my chest. I've dreamed of him saying that to me for so long.

That's what this is. A dream.

The best dream.

One I never want to wake from.

I swallow again, gaze into his eyes, and swoon. "I'm happy I'm here too."

Both sides of his lips raise, and I ponder if this is my favorite smile yet. It's hard to decide as all his smiles are his best smiles. "Did you know I had the biggest crush on you in high school?"

"Ah, no. I couldn't tell." The breath rings out of my chest. "You never said anything, other than that time you asked me to save a dance for you."

"Right." He nodded, his movement so smooth, and easy. "I was shy. That obviously didn't do anything but waste a lot of time." He raised his hand, touching my chin lightly with the pads of his fingers.

So much time! I scream in my head. It's been years!

"I assumed you thought I was Rocco's annoying little sister."

His fingers graze my chin as he lowers his lips closer, parting them in the slowest speed setting.

I'm unable to make a sound but my lips part. Drawing his chin even closer to me, the warmth wafts off his skin.

It's surreal.

It's serendipity.

It's our most romantic moment, and I don't ever want it to end. I start to close my eyes and lean in, but he tips his head up and softly presses a smile on my forehead.

Is this right?

Time literally stills as we hold each other – *not kissing. Why aren't we kissing?*

After so many several long moments, I wonder if we are frozen before he reaches for my hand, lacing his fingers into mine. Yes that part is amazing, but *it's not kissing!*

"How about that coffee?" he asks like this is the most casual encounter ever.

"Coffee is always a yes." I force a grin with my un-kissed lips. I don't even have to ask where we're going because he's a man of routines, and his routine is the Coffee Loft.

Thirteen

North

Sitting across from each other at the same Coffee Loft booth—me drinking my ol' reliable spiced chai, and Gia risking a blueberry mocha—our free hands slide across the table until they meet, and we playfully hold hands like two giddy teenagers.

Gia dips her drink straw into the mountain of whip cream, scoops a glop up, and then brings it to her mouth. I fight the urge to hang my jaw as this might be the most entertaining thing I've seen all year, and I coach football for a living, so I see an awful lot of entertaining things. Need I say more?

"I'm still in so much disbelief over this last week." Her voice is relaxed and smokey, as if we've finally broken all the nervous jitters we've had between us for the last...well forever.

"I've enjoyed this week so much." I make sure to close my jaw, securely fastening it into place, but find myself biting my lower lip.

As she sips from her straw, I slide to the edge of my seat, my gaze glued to her lips. My own lips tingle as if they feel hers on them. "Let me ask you something." She shifts in her seat, leaning back, relaxing even more. "If you liked me in high school, why didn't you ever say anything?

One word—or rather one big aerodynamic face—flashes through my mind.

Rocco.

I don't dare tell her that her brother had threatened me to stay away, because it will upset her. She already has such an emotional time talking about Rocco. She doesn't need to know another way he potentially destroyed her happiness. I shrug a shoulder, but it does nothing to ease the tension that Rocco's name instills in my body. "Ah, I've always been shy, especially when it comes to you."

"Right, back then." She drags an index finger in the air, as if to motion to the past. "But this week you haven't been shy at all. What changed?"

"I guess the fact that I saw how fast time goes. I figured if you rejected me, I could just avoid you. It's not like you live next door anymore." I reach across the table and grab her other hand. Even holding both hands, I still don't feel close enough. "And because it had to be for something. Someone doesn't hold onto that kind of chemistry for so long if it doesn't matter."

"I know you like your routines." Her eyebrow spikes to challenge me. "Hanging out with me may *mess* all those up."

"To be honest," I slap on my mischievous smile. "all I ever wanted was you to mess up my life."

Her lashes flutter, and I bring her hand to my lips, dropping a chaste kiss on her hand.

It's the most amazing feeling to be able to do that.

Better than winning *any* football game.

Well, maybe not the super bowl, but let's be realistic in our comparisons.

Better than winning any *high school* football game.

Her cheeks flush, and she looks down at her phone. "I think they're going to close soon, but I'm at my dad's all weekend. You're welcome to come on over."

We rise to our feet at the same time, meandering to the door like we've been in sync for years. I walk her all the way to her car and give her my most natural smile. "My car is in staff parking, so I'll say goodnight here." I don't think it's too soon to risk a kiss, but I'm just savoring the sweetness we have right now. I lean in, wrap my arms around her for a long hug. It already feels like we've belonged together forever. When I pull away, I open her car door and say, "Night."

She plops down onto the driver's seat, smiling in a way that brightens her already glowing face. "Night, North."

I close the door and stand with both hands in my jacket pockets as she drives out of the parking lot, and then I stroll back to my car, whistling *My Girl* the whole way.

I round the corner, and notice my car is the only one left in the employee lot, but I'm not alone. A dark figure paces around my car, causing me to squint, and bring him into clearer focus. I understand the presence is no accident, nor coincidence.

Ice floods my veins, and I slow my steps until we're standing face to face. "Rocco."

He stops in front of my driver's door, blocking my car. His shaved head glimmers under the streetlight, and he's dressed like he's in the mob or something in his ominous monotone black. He's always had a flare for the dramatic. "Well, look at you. Hometown football coach hero, winning the game at the last second."

"What do you want?" My fingers dig into my palms. I'm not afraid of him. I can hold my own. Rocco has never been about physical violence. He always aims deeper than that—the pocketbook.

"Who says I want anything?"

"Well, it's almost ten o'clock." I struggle not to put my fist in his fat smug lip. "You're out here pacing an empty parking lot."

"I thought we could chat." His nostrils flare, tipping me off that he's lying. "With it being near the end of the year, and everything, I was looking through some tax stuff, and we need to talk about my sponsorship check for next year—"

"Cut to the chase," I speak over him. "It's Friday night. This isn't about your check. What do you want?"

He pulls out his phone, flashing something at me on his screen. "Want to explain what this is." He snarls.

My gaze centers on his phone.

A photo of Gia and me holding each other under the bleachers.

"I told you to leave my sister alone. Did I not?"

I scoff. *He can't be serious!* "We were kids, Rocco." I shake my head at how preposterous this is. "She's an adult now, and so am I. This is crazy. Can you please step aside so I can get in my car?"

Shoving his phone in his pocket, he narrows his gaze, resentment etching the tips of his lips. "You seem to forget; I never *asked*. You will stay away from her, or you will pay."

Pay.

That's exactly what he's after. Blackmail of some sort, but joke's on him, I'm a teacher. I don't have any money. The only thing he can possibly take from me is that sponsorship check, but the whole town counts on that. He'd only be hurting himself.

The thing with Rocco is he is too stupid to see that. He'd be the guy who would destroy his own livelihood if it meant he could take down someone he hates. Every fiber of my being knows he isn't bluffing, but I've spent my life afraid of Rocco.

I'm so done having him bully me. My entire life I've cowered from his threats. It's gotten me nowhere.

I'm done being that guy.

Anger buds from my gut, burning a spiral of adrenaline through all my extremities. My fingers tighten one by one into a tight fist, and I slowly pull my hand back, winding up. The sequence plays out in slow motion, and it's everything I've wanted to do to Rocco for years. With the deepest breath I can suck in, I dream of slugging him in his gut. Instead, I take the higher road, push past him, bumping my shoulder into his. "Get lost," I murmur and I steal the opportunity to slide into my car. I don't even check the rearview mirror as I squeal the tires and speed off.

I've never felt better.

Fourteen

Gia

"Dad." My palm frantically finds the dash while my other hand secures the door handle. "You need to let me drive."

He putters forward in his old red Ford. It's not his speed that is making my heart screech in my chest, but his lack of sense of space. We're on our way to Bella's for lunch and to grab the daily deposit. That part is dandy and sounds like a nice little Saturday. The part that's aging me faster than a banana in an oven is he's *nearly* clipped every car parked on the side of the road.

"There's nothing wrong with my driving." He slams on the old, squeaky, disc brakes. With only the lap belts holding us down, we both swing forward at the waist.

This is worse than Space Mountain Roller Coaster!

Cars stack up behind us, serial honking.

This is where it all ends! I'm clearly going to die!

"You're lucky you don't have GPS in this old thing, because instead of giving directions, it would be rattling off prayers!" I scream out as I frantically swipe my hand through my hair, pulling it behind my ears, resisting the urge to yank it all out.

"Ah, those GPSLMNOPs robots these days are overrated." He puts his blinker on to turn left but then proceeds to take a *right* on red.

"Dad!" I grab his wheel, yanking it hard to the right to dodge oncoming traffic. "You had the wrong blinker on!" He slams on the brake, halting us in the middle of the road. Again.

Beeeeep! A double-decker tour bus nearly sideswipes as it wails past, and icy sweat frosts my forehead.

"We are in the middle of the road." Tossing a look behind me, traffic is lined up down the next block, and mortification washes my face with a warm flush. "Move, Dad!" I hastily wave for him to pull forward.

"Hold on." He guns us out into traffic. Sweat pours down my brow, and my shoulders hug my ears as tension pulls them together. When he rounds the final corner, he finds a metered spot in front of the pizzeria, I let out the biggest sigh of relief.

A series of chuckles radiates from Dad's lips.

"How can you laugh?" I give him a stoney glare.

"I long since learned not to cry in times of stress."

"It wouldn't have been stressful if you'd let me drive in the first place."

"True." He tips his head toward me. "But then we'd have nothing to laugh about."

"It's not funny." I let out a huff as I tug on the door handle to let myself out. "Plus, now I need to ruin my diet, because the only thing that's going to help me is a giant cup of diabetes."

"You should try that new Coffee shop." He winks at me as he hops out of the truck onto the busy sidewalk.

My gaze skirts to the other side of the street where I see the Coffee Loft. It's the breath of fresh air I need. I tap my chin only one time before I give into the temptation. "I think I want to do that. Do you mind if I run over and grab a coffee and meet you back here for pizza? You can order, and I'll be right in."

"I don't have a problem with that." Dad wobbles forward to the pizzeria.

Dodging traffic, I dart out as soon as it's clear, and I make it across the street in a few seconds flat. As always, I slow my steps right as I pass through the front door, and deep roasted cinnamon wafts under my nose. It's impossible to not feel rejuvenated when I'm in this place. The lady working behind the counter smiles in full recognition and waves. "Welcome to the Coffee Loft. What can I grab you today?"

With so many options, it's impossible to choose. "What flavor pairs well with three hours of sleep and a near-death driving situation?"

"May I suggest the French Press?" Her lashes bat as she looks back at the man behind her who rolls his eyes at her. I suspect some serious flirtation and it puts a smile on my face.

"That sounds perfect. Lofty size, please."

While she gets busy scooping coffee into the French press, she starts small talk. "Is the sun still shining out there?"

"A little bit." I nod, adding, "Starting to get windy though, but considering it's fall, I'm happy."

"Right? We never have this much sunshine in November." She pours hot water in the French press, and sets it aside on the counter before returning to the tablet. "Is that everything, or do you need a spiced chai for North?" She grins slyly at me, winking.

"I ah, don't know. I suppose I can grab one, and he can heat it up later. I haven't talked to him yet today." My cheeks burn as I ramble. I hadn't expected people to assume we were together, but after recalling how we sat practically cuddling in the booth last night, I can understand why she thought that. "Was he here yet?"

"No." She shakes her head back and forth. "Normally, he stops in after his morning run on Saturdays, but no sign of him today. That's why I thought you were grabbing for both of you."

"Well." I open my purse, and dig for my debit card, excitement budding in my gut. I can't wait to be able to surprise him with his 'coffee' order. "You better add a spiced chai to my order, please."

"You bet." She punches in the second order. "Spiced chai coming right up!"

I swipe, and quickly stow my card, and while she's working on North's drink, I scroll my phone. No text messages from him. He'd been texting me almost every morning since we cleaned the garage. But not today.

For a guy who clings to his routines, it seems odd he's so off schedule.

The barista slides a drink carrier with the two drinks across the bar. "I put stoppers in them, so they stay warm."

"Thank you." I take the carrier by the handle and head out, noting it's only been about ten minutes. Dad usually spends at least thirty minutes talking before he remembers he's actually there to eat, he likely hasn't even ordered yet.

I push open the heavy door, taking a big stride out, hoping to rush back across the street in record time, when I nearly run smack into someone. "Pardon me." I startle, trying to steady my drink carrier. Thanks to the stoppers every drop is spared. I smile and raise my gaze.

My stomach instantly knots, and I squeak out, "Rocco. Hi."

"Hey, lil sis." His face is stilled, not wavering into even the tiniest smile. It's been months, if not even a year or two since I've seen him, but he has his shaved head, which highlights his oversized nose. It's identical to dad's nose, but oddly while it makes Dad look endearing, it gives Rocco's face a disproportionate effect. Cloaked in a long trench coat that stops above his shiny black shoes, he's definitely dressed for business.

I just can't tell if it's legal business or not.

"H-how are you?"

"I'm fantastic." With precisely measured words, he doesn't break direct eye contact. "I actually just completed the final steps to run for Senate."

Senate? Boy, that really is where all the crooks go.

Biting my lips, I offer nothing. But running for Senate doesn't surprise me. He's always doing everything to gain more power and control.

"I didn't realize you were in town." He offers after the silence drags out. "It's been a while."

"It's been a looong time." I nod, feeling as if I'm shrinking in size right in the middle of the sidewalk.

"How have you been?" Pulling his hands out of his pockets, he extends his arms wide, and waves me forward for a hug.

It feels off.

Rocco and I never had a close relationship even before fame and money ruined him, but I don't have an excuse not to hug him. I shuffle the drink carrier into one hand and lean in sideways for the world's fastest hug. "I'm well. Just back for the weekend. Helping Dad clean out his house."

Angling his head toward me, he echoes, "Cleaning it out? Where's he going?"

"Nowhere. His clutter has gotten out of hand." I gesture with an open palm forward. "You know how he is with his collections."

"Right." His lips thin into a straight line.

"Well." I jerk my thumb over my shoulder toward the pizzeria, careful with my words not to accidentally invite him to lunch. "I need to go."

"Oh." He nods, planting a smirk on his face. "Sorry to bother you."

"It's no bother. Just have plans." I wave as politely as I can, my skin crawling with the creeps, and I can't rush across the street fast enough.

My mind is a whirlwind as I stare down at my coffees.

North, the man with the world's most routines is off routine.

And Rocco's running for the senate.

What next?

Fifteen

North

The next morning, I'm in my kitchen, staring at Mr. Bella's junk box still sitting neatly in the corner of my kitchen table. Not wanting to snoop, I had left it untouched after seeing Rocco's football poster. Now I want to grab the whole box and chuck it out the front door in hopes that something valuable of Rocco's smashes into a million pieces.

Anger fires in my chest. I can't believe Rocco had the *audacity* to threaten my football team, which is my livelihood over me spending time with Gia.

I'm not fourteen.

I have no ill intentions toward Gia.

I've literally loved her my entire life.

All I want to do is love and protect her in the way she deserves.

He's the monster who needs to be taught a lesson.

If he thinks I'm giving up this easily, after all the years I've pined over Gia, well, he has another thing to learn. I may be a little slow to make my move, but when I put my mind to something, I'm in one thousand percent.

Gia's always been in my head.

She's always consumed my heart.

But now, she's in my life and I'm not giving that up.

Knock, knock.

My gaze skirts to the front door. I had been so wrapped up in my head, I missed Gia crossing the yard. She stands on my front porch, looking more amazing than ever. Her hair is up in one of the homeless messy buns she wears that looks hot. She's wearing an oversized, washed-out Bulldogs sweater. I know for a fact she's had it since high school, because she used to wear it to cheerleading practice. I'd always fight it, but many days they'd practice on the edge of the football field when we were running scrimmages. There was no way I could ever keep my eyes off her. Seeing her wear that sweatshirt after all these years sets an explosion of sparks right to my heart. It's like a symbol that it's finally our time to be together, and all those years wasted in unrequited love are about to pay off.

I push open the door, and her cute button nose wrinkles from the smile on her face. "Hey, you." I step aside, motioning for her to come inside. "What a nice surprise."

She offers me one of two cups in her hands. "Coffee Loft spiced chai, just the way you like it."

"I could get used to this service." I take the drink and immediately enjoy a sip. It's lukewarm, but still delicious.

"I was downtown with Dad for lunch, so I stopped in. Portia mentioned you broke your routine and hadn't come in for your morning coffee. I know how you are with routines, and it made me a little concerned." Her gorgeous green eyes travel over my face. "Is everything okay?

"Yeah." I pause, not wanting to lie to her. I'm an overly honest person, but I don't want to cause her to worry. I certainly don't want to give her a reason to pause *us*. I nonchalantly pat my abs. "My stomach is having sort of an off day. I hadn't left the house yet."

"That's no good."

I wave, dismissing her concern. "If I had to diagnose this, I'd say it was mostly related to butterflies." That earns me a raised feathered eyebrow and a flirty smile, and I tack on, "I have no idea what species they are, but they moved in last weekend, and it's clear they're taking over."

My heart swells from her joyful giggles, and we lock our gazes and stand frozen. The corners of her eyes crinkle in the cutest way as she retorts back, "I'm afraid they aren't butterflies."

"They aren't?"

"Nope, not for you. You're more special. You have little baby axolotls in there, hopping around."

"I do?" Our laughter mingles together perfectly in sync. "I think you're right. That's exactly what I have."

She takes a step further into my kitchen, glancing around. "It's been years since I've been here. Not much has changed, huh?"

"Nope. When my parents moved, I left everything exactly as it was. You know me." I wink and shoot a playful finger gun at her. "I like routines."

As she continues to look around, she tosses me a smile that transforms her face. It's flirty, but yet it has the sort of expression that says she's testing me.

I step behind her. "Are you looking for something specific?"

"Nah, just seeing what your life is like."

I casually extend my arm, ushering her further in. "You're welcome to take a tour. Mi casa es su casa."

"Oh." Her eyes round, glinting with bright green specs. "Are we at that stage already?"

"Baby," I tease, my voice lower than normal. "I'll meet you at any stage you want. You tell me. What stage are we at?"

She holds my gaze, and I don't waver as I'm ready to see this through.

She's all I ever wanted.

Her teeth dig into her plush bottom lip, flushing it to a darker pink, and I can literally see the wheels turning in her pretty little head. The anticipation of her next words makes those stomach axolotls come alive. They're gearing up to swim a marathon. She can say anything, and I will agree.

Does she want to be my girlfriend?

Yeah, I'm there.

Heck, does she want to get engaged?

I will *run* to the jewelry store with bare feet.

Would she prefer to skip the engagement and get married?

Vegas, here we come!

I don't want to close my eyes, but if I do, all I will ever see is her beautiful face etched into my brain.

Because it's already been there forever.

She's etched into my soul.

"Gia," I whisper, my voice growing with concern because she hasn't answered me yet. "What do you think this is?"

"I didn't think we were allowed to put a label on it yet." Her cadence is slow, as if she is weighing each word carefully before allowing it to make a sound.

My heart deflates. That doesn't sound like someone who's all in. Maybe she's not ready?

"*We* don't need a label," I rush to downplay everything. My inflections mirror her cautionary ones. "But I want you to know I've enjoyed spending time with you."

Her lashes flutter, the way they always do when she's trying to avoid blushing. "Me, too."

"Good," I assert, pulling my lips in, and biting hard, as it's a struggle. Her hesitation to put a label on us makes me think she might not be ready yet.

A horrible thought enters my brain. What if she's just being nice to me so I'll help her clean out all that junk? Even if that is the case, I offered to help, and I'm a man of my word. I jerk my thumb over my shoulder at the door. "What do you say, I help you clean another stack of boxes?"

"Well, I'm hoping to take a load of boxes to the dump. Would you want to help with that?"

"Yeah." I slip on my tennis shoes and grab my keys. "Let's go throw out some trash." Loving how the least desirable chore in the world can feel like I won the lottery when I get to be next to Gia, I'm unable to stop grinning as we stroll through the door together, and head back across the yard toward Mr. Bella's loaded-down-with-junk truck.

It only takes about an hour to drop everything off, and when we return, we spend the rest of the day cleaning more boxes. This time we find a stamp collection, and something a little odd, an assortment of dog toys—even though Gia swears they never owned a pet. That discovery made us both burst into fits of laughter, and just like all the other days we'd worked, time got away from us, and it's time for me to go home.

With Mr. Bella lingering in the kitchen, we say a quick goodnight, and I head across the yard to my house.

What do you know, I'm not alone.

Rocco's wringing his hands together, blocking my front door. "Well, well, well . . ." His sinister grin cements on his face. "Tell me this isn't what it looks like."

Grinding my back teeth together, I fight back every urge I have to flatten his smug expression. As good as it would feel to hit him, that's not going to solve anything. He clearly didn't get the hint that I'm not giving up Gia.

My hands shake, but I squeeze my fist into a ball and stuff it in my jacket—for now.

I'm not going to let him control me—or Gia anymore.

"Look," I growl. "If Gia doesn't want me around, she's perfectly capable of letting me know that herself. She doesn't need you butting in. I'm sorry if that hurts your tiny feelings."

Rocco's head rolls back, and a haughty laugh pipes out for an egregious amount of time before he finally forms actual words. "We will see who's sorry." His eyes narrow into slits before he spins on his heel and strides to his black car, parked at an angle in my driveway, blocking me in.

If this were a movie, the only thing that would have been missing is the evil mustache twirl before he stormed off. I have no idea how he got this way, but that man is delusional. I'm not above calling the cops if it gets to that level, but I just hate to do anything rash that will upset Gia. He may not be able to keep me away, but there's burning in the back of my brain telling me he will do something.

I clear my throat and steel my shoulders back in the door-way. "You want to see me, Principal Lane?"

"Yes. Come on in." Principal Lane swivels on his computer chair to face me while gesturing to the chair in front of his desk. It's Monday morning, and first period is just about to begin, but I had an urgent message to come here. "Have a seat, please."

Principal Lane leans back in his chair and adjusts his beige sport coat collar to lay flat against the high-back leather chair. His suit is practically the same color as his hair, his mustache, and his skin tone. It's so monotone, it makes it hard for me to find his face, but he's always worn this color. "I'm afraid I've had some bad news about the football budget. Our biggest sponsor, Rocco's Motors Company, has not renewed their sponsorship for next year."

"Wh-what?" I stammer and jump to my feet, searching for something—anything—on this desk or computer screen that has evidence this isn't some practical joke. Rocco mentioned pulling support, but I didn't think that he actually meant it. His ego was making the threats. Swallowing down my shock, I look Principal Lane in the eye. "What was his reasoning?"

"He's had a change of priorities. He said he's running for Senate and wants to use his philanthropy funds towards more humanitarian missions, such as feeding and clothing the homeless. He did say he feels terrible because the town's gotten used to his hefty donation, but he said it was God's calling."

Nearly choking on my own tongue, I fight every urge to explode with the truth.

This is no spiritual awakening.

This is revenge.

Principal Lane didn't need to know about my personal life, and how I might have caused this, but there must be some more details. "So, um," I stretch my neck forward, already feeling the strain of this financial burden move into my body. "What are we looking at for cuts? Do the boosters have a plan, or fundraiser?"

"The boosters haven't been doing a whole lot other than the Homecoming auction and raffle. Rocco's made their job easy, but I'm not going to abandon you, and it's early. I'm sure we can plan something. A good car wash fundraiser, and perhaps the guys could sell those pizzas the cheerleaders always sell?"

"Right." My mouth dries up. Selling frozen pizzas is not going to come close to replacing the money that Rocco donated.

"Effective immediately, we'll have to eliminate assistant coach, Rod, from the payroll, and we'll do our best to keep your hours as is. However, we're in need of some major fundraising and possibly cold calling businesses for donations."

I nod, and then nod again, because I know if I open my mouth, I'll have some choice words to say about Rocco. I zip my lips as I don't want to say anything I'll regret. "I'm sorry to hear this, but hopefully it's only a minor setback. We'll figure something out." I rise and offer a handshake. "Thanks for keeping me in the loop and let me know when more news arises."

"Will do." Principal Lane finally grips my hand, shaking it extra *firmly.* "We'll see your boys out on the field again Friday night. This won't faze them."

"Sure thing." I fake a toothy smile and pivot to exit his office. I know one thing. As much as I hate this, I'm going to need to tell Gia. It's way beyond a coincidence, and I need to warn her to watch her back. My cell vibrates in my pocket. I never get calls during the day. Everyone knows I'm at school. My gut clenches before I even look.

I duck into my classroom, as I have ten minutes before the first period starts, and I close the door.

Rocco: I warned you. Stay away or you'll *both* be sorry.

Both.

That has to be a typo. He can't mean us both. Would he really hurt his own sister?

Stunned, I stare at the wall as if the air is too poisoned for it to be stirred. It definitely is blackmail. Rocco and his dirty friends are behind all of this, and I must find a way to stop him, and warn Gia.

Gia, my heart slams against my chest. I can't have him going after her. I must protect her at all costs until I can find a way to stop him for good.

It's like he has some super GPS on us, and spies everywhere. He just knows when we are together. I rub my chin, hating that I have to tell Gia this bad news, but it must be done. I've held off telling her long enough. She needs to know everything.

Seventeen

Gia

"Sorry I'm late!" I yank my heavy coat off, and neatly toss it on the coat hook as I breeze by it. The aroma of thyme and fresh basil tickles my nose, awakening me. Grace is already aproned up and spacing cinnamon roll dough on the pans, something I usually do. I grab an apron, quickly tie it around my waist, and scoot in front of the handwashing sink to scrub. "Let me do the rolls."

"It's fine." She plops the last of the dough on the pan and whisks the bowl into the soaking sink. "I already have all my roasts in the convection oven."

"That's what smells so hearty." I stick my nose high in the air, inhaling one more time.

"Yes, I used all the leftover onions." She pauses and her eyebrows clamp together, tipping me off to her confusion.

"So, get this. An administrative meeting is going on in the brunch room."

"An admin meeting on a Monday morning?" I echo, my Spidey sense alerting. "As long as I've been here, they've always stuck to Thursday lunches."

"Right? It felt off to me, too. It was deathly quiet when I walked in this morning, and the curtain dividing those two dining rooms had been rolled back. I thought maybe the weekend staff never closed it. I went in there to tidy up, and that's when I saw Gerry, and Marcie. It's both of their mornings off, but they had gotten emails last night, announcing an emergency meeting this morning."

"That doesn't sound good." I swallow, bustling to the kitchen door to peek out the window into the dining room, all the seats at the round center table are filled with management. All their faces are devoid of expression. "Are we supposed to go to this meeting?"

"Nobody said." She slides her pans into the oven and joins me, standing on her toes to look inside. "It doesn't look like we're getting huge bonuses, does it?"

"Nope."

"I don't know." She drops to her flat feet, brushing off her apron. "I can't imagine it's anything *bad*. The holidays are right around the corner, and it's our busiest season."

"Do you know what? I bet that's what it's actually all about." I breathe out, hoping to convince myself that this isn't going to negatively affect my position, or my pay.

"Maybe we are going to be so busy, they need to implement some new schedule?"

I back away from the window as Marcie rises from her seat and heads our way. I push open the swinging door for her, and a look of dread consumes her face.

"What's the meeting about?" I ask so softly I can barely hear my own voice.

"We got shut down." Marcie exhales, disbelief in all her facial features. Even her perfect perky-Karen haircut seems to be deflated today.

"What?" My T ticks hard and I stammer, "Wh-what do you mean?"

Her gaze waffles between Grace and me. "They pulled our hospitality license, citing health and safety concerns. The guests are all being asked to check out this morning, and as soon as they have vacated, we lock up."

"I don't believe it." My jaw hangs low, and I rack my brain for clues. "Did something happen over the weekend? I don't even remember any inspectors coming around."

"We were never notified about anything." Marcie shrugs hard, her whole face falls with her shoulders. "It almost seems like sabotage. This is a high-demand beachfront property. Some businessman is probably trying to get this place to foreclose so they can buy it on the cheap."

"That's crazy." My voice pitches higher, anger filling my chest. "Who would do that?" Goosebumps rip over my arms, and the hair on my arms stands straight up. I gulp, scanning the kitchen with tears stinging my eyes. This has been my entire life since high school. It's not a perfect job, and I'm not getting rich, but Grace is like a sister to me, and food service is really all I know.

"Ah, it's going to be okay." Grace rushes over and wraps her arms around me. I hadn't realized Grace was also tearing up. Speaking through her sniffles, she tacks on, "We'll figure something out together."

"Yeah," I assure us both. "We'll find something else much better than this."

A niggling in the back of my head haunts me.

Who would want to sabotage this hotel?

Eighteen

North

I stop by the Coffee Loft on my way home from practice, my brain still abuzz with Rocco's threats. While I wait for my spiced chai, my phone vibrates with a text.

Gia: How was work?

My fingers itch to type back but my heart knows this must pause. Not forever, but until I can find a way to stop Rocco, or she'll get hurt. I'm not worth losing anything for. After several moments of staring at my phone and not texting back, she sends another text.

Gia: So crazy thing . . . I guess I'm staying at my dad's house tonight. The hotel got shut down unexpectedly. I'm going to finish cleaning the house. If you're around, come over. You don't have to clean. LOL

Anger boils in my gut and I fire off a text.

Me: What? Was it foreclosed?

Gia: No. The health inspector shut us down, but I don't even remember being inspected. It's really odd. My boss thought it was sabotage to buy up the prime real estate.

Sabotage or revenge?

Did Rocco pull something to shut it down? It wouldn't surprise me, and he has the means to do it with all his buddies on political favor payroll. Which means he already got to her. I can literally hear her sweet voice. I want to protect her. It feels like a knife is stabbing my gut to even think about someone hurting her. Now I'm torn. Do I stay away and hope he backs down? Hope isn't a plan, and it's clearly not working.

I'm not sure how I'm going to stay away. I certainly don't want to alarm her before I have the proof of harassment, I need in order to call the cops. Until I get that proof, I need to have her stay away.

Me: I'm really sorry about your job. I'm sure something amazing will come along. I'll see if I can get my work done and get ahold of you later.

I fight the urge to tell her I know exactly how she's feeling as I had my job nearly threatened today too. All I want to do is see her. The fact that she's going to be next door tonight is going to kill me, but I can't waste time. I need to gather my proof. There's something shady going on at the school. I have no idea how Rocco got to Principal Lane so fast. I stuff my phone in my pocket, grab my chai and head back to school. I have work to do.

The hairs on my arm stand up straight when I park in the employee parking lot, hours after dark. It's not unusual for teachers to return to their classroom to work, as we are all trying to get ahead, but tonight, it looks as if I'm the only one taking a second shift. As I exit my car and walk to the door, I jingle my keys in my hand, my senses alerted.

No sign of Rocco or Principal Lane.

Or at least no sign that I can see.

After unlocking the door, I slip inside and quickly lock it behind me, before flipping on several sets of lights. To deal with the silence, I whistle down the hall to my classroom. I'm not a musician and barely know any tunes, but automatically default to *My Girl*. A smile teases at the corner of my lips as I recall how it felt to hold Gia while we danced.

It will not be the last time I hold her.

I grind my molars while I unlock my classroom door. Maxlotle's aquarium is already glowing fluorescent, lighting up the back of the room. Still, I flip on another set of lights. "Hey, Buddy." I only speak out loud to him when I know we are alone. It's good for him to hear my voice, but I always feel looney doing it in front of people. "What are you up to tonight?"

He swims to the front, his perma-smile pressing up against the glass. I don't think anyone could ever be grumpy around an axolotl. "Well," I continue as if he can fully understand me—because I know he can. "I'm in a bit of a pickle. There's this woman, you met her the other day, Gia. I'm heartsick over her, because I really thought we could finally be together, but her brother is doing everything he can to keep us apart." I rub my forehead, as my tension automatically pools there. This all seems so ridiculous. The part about Rocco keeping us apart. Not me talking to a salamander. That's completely sane. "What do you think I should do?"

He stares at me through the glass with his beady eyes, not blinking. He's looking past me now, back to my desk.

"That's what I thought. I need to get into Principal Lane's office. I'm sure there's something on his computer to prove things aren't right." I get up, pooling my bravery as I trudge my way to my desk to look for a file, or something I can use to get into his office, when my gaze snags on something.

Gia's box of Rocco's stuff.

It's still sitting on the corner of my desk. I haven't really wanted to look at his trophies and jerseys as anything of Rocco's makes me ill. I only took the box to make her happy, but now seeing it there infuriates me. After all these years of doing everything I could to cut him out of my life, he has managed to creep back in, and now has more control than ever before. It's not just Gia he wants to keep me from, now he's after my career and her job.

What next? Is he going to get my teaching license taken away? It's never going to end!

My fingers wrap into a tight fist, and I plot what to do with his trophies. I could smash them all up. It will feel amazing, but make a mess that I will have to clean. I really don't want to give him any more of my time. Dropping it in the trash would be the easiest way to get rid of it. It's dark out. Nobody would even see the box inside, and the garbage truck will take it away.

But what if Gia wants to see them someday?

What will I tell her?

I can't lie to her.

I also know I can't sit at my desk and look at this dumb box. The mere thought of him being in my life makes my frustration soar through my entire body, and I rip open the flaps, ready to deal with what's inside. I can stash this stuff in the corner of the locker room and just never go there. I'll keep my promise to Gia and get rid of it all at the same time.

"Alright." I sigh again, summoning the strength to deal with this. "What do I have here?"

I yank out the first trophy. A 12-inch plastic pedestal with a football on top. The plaque reads: Rookie of the year.

Cute, I mock and grab the next one.

Most valuable player.

Gag me.

Maybe I don't need to read them? Just grab them and go. I close one eye, as I go in for another, but my fingers brush up against a manila envelope.

Oh, what is this? Fancy certificates? Shaking my head, pushing them off, I vow to pretend I never saw them. I'm sure not framing anything.

A panic niggling in the back of my head screams at me, *You better check this.*

Really? I sigh again and impatiently grab the envelope, rip it open, and my eyes immediately swell round.

This isn't an award.

Mr. Bella clearly had *everything.*

Including these original loan papers for Rocco's car lot.

I would think Rocco would want these in his office, because it has all his personal information, and because he's shady as an oak tree, my interest is full throttle. I flip through the papers, and the hair on my arms rises again.

Something is immediately off.

Principal Lane's signature is next to Rocco's as a co-owner, alongside Tom Schank, president of the school board, and one of the shadiest businessmen in the town. He used to work in education but now he sits on several of the most influencial boards in town and owns a string of hotels.

Hotels.

Might he own Gia's hotel?

Ice frosts my back, spiraling chills to creep up my spine as I scan loan papers. Underneath the bank papers is another letter, a printed email from Rocco to Principal Lane. I speed read it with my heart nearly pumping out of my heart. I can't believe what I'm reading but *everything* becomes unveiled. Tom bought Rocco and Principal's vote for all these boards he's on. Tom basically owns them both as Tom is the one who gave Rocco money for his car lot, and in exchange for that, Rocco had to agree to sponsor the football team, which apparently was a condition Principal Lane made.

They are in on this together.

I smash my lips together and keep reading, as it all makes so much sense. That's how Rocco got to Principal Lane so fast. He's blackmailable. Swallowing hard, I stuff the papers back in the envelope and scan my room.

Still eerily quiet, but I have what I need to out Rocco now. That these papers landed in my hands at the exact time I need them is a miracle, but I'm not going to bury them. I protected Rocco when I found out about his cheating, but it got me nowhere. I'm done with him. Rocco's going to jail, and I'll be able to see Gia. Adrenaline surges, as I slide the envelope in a book bag, wanting to conceal it. To think, I almost threw it in the trash.

I stride out of my classroom, shut off the lights, and lock my door. I must get to Gia and tell Mr. Bella before it's too late, and Rocco does something else.

Oddly, Mr. Bella had the smoking gun to take down Rocco this whole time. It's weird it would end up in this box, without him knowing it.

Or did he know?

Nineteen

Gia

Peering out Dad's window for the third time in the last five minutes, I crane my neck.

Still no car in the driveway.

I wonder what North is doing. Going out on a Monday night is against his normal routine, but it's a little too soon in our situationship for me to demand he tell me what he's up to.

He was awfully vague.

What if he's on a date?

Nah—I cut my thoughts off, and then immediately remember he was the one who rushed to say we don't need a label for our relationship. At the time, I assumed he was being shy, but maybe that was to cover up something else?

Would he really date someone else?

He also didn't kiss me when he had the chance.

Again, I thought he was being shy.

What if he really isn't interested, and I've been misreading him the whole time? He said he went out of his way to be a friend to Rocco when he got in trouble. What if he's just a nice guy, trying to be a friend to me, because he saw my dad get stuck.

To be honest, he hasn't ever asked me out on a proper date. We've only grabbed coffee and tea from the Coffee Loft and cleaned. If he is truly interested, he'd take me to dinner or a movie. Right?

"Gia!" Dad calls as he walks through the front door, pizza in his arms. "I'm so sorry to hear about your day."

"It's okay. Just a job. It's probably time I move on anyway. I was at a bit of standstill with my career." Closing the window curtain, I hang my head, sulk into the kitchen, and pull up a chair at the table while I wait for dad to bring over the pizza.

He drops the box in the center of the table and flips open the lid. Pepperoni and jalapeño—my favorite. Not waiting for a plate, I dig right in, help myself to a nice cheesy slice and take a giant bite.

Dad mirrors me, plopping in the chair across from me, and grabs a slice. "I was thinking," he says while he chews down his food. "You can help me in the pizzeria."

"Dad." I sigh, as I really don't need him to offer me a pity job.

"No, hear me out." He places his hand on mine. "I've been enjoying my house being so clean. It's so freeing, and in a way it feels like I've gotten a new chance at life." His voice cracks, and I stop mid-chew. I knew he was dealing with heavy emotions, but he hasn't opened up to me about it yet, other than the arguments we've had about not throwing out his stuff. "After your mom died, and Rocco got in all that trouble, I just sort of wanted to hide."

"I know, Dad." I match my gaze with his. "I've never faulted you for any of this mess. We were all doing the best we could."

"Well, but I do think I'm better now." His eyes are bright and clear, clueing me in to his honesty. "But, I'm tired, and I want a break. When North's parents sold that house to him, they retired to Mexico City. They invited me to visit, and you know, I think it sounds nice."

"Oh." Tipping my head to the side, I let that sink in. "I had no idea you needed a break. Of course, I can cover for you. How long are we talking about?" I take another bite, and chew.

"I'm awfully sick of the cold. My bones don't handle it like they used to. I've been thinking about it for a while, but never had a way to swing it. If you think you can cover for me, I'd like to leave soon. Maybe give you a week to train you back in as it's been years since you covered a shift, and I'll make the arrangements. I'd love to stay until spring." He jerks a thumb over his shoulder, pointing down the hall. "You can stay here in your old bedroom. I know you have a couple of months left on your lease, but by all means, if you want to let it go at the end of the year, you're more than welcome to crash until you get settled into a new job."

I swallow the last of my pizza, but really, I'm swallowing more than that. I'm so overly touched that Dad thought this all out before I had a chance to get worried about my bills.

"And," Dad cuts into my thoughts. "If you find a job you want to take before spring, just holler and I'll be right back."

"I love you, Dad," I say, the words spilling out as tears fall. Tears that I hadn't even realized were hiding back here, but these last two weeks have been such a whirlwind. Swiping my eyes with the back of my hand, I lean over and wrap my arms around his neck. He hugs me back, and I inhale the scent of fresh oregano and pepper—the scent he's always worn since he works at the pizza shop. I bite back a smile, knowing this is going to be my new scent.

"Say," Dad says while finishing his pizza and brushing off the last of the crusts into the open box. "I want to show you something." He stands and starts walking down the hall. "You'll never guess what I found . . ." His voice trickles off as he enters into Rocco's room. When he pops back out with a toddler sized, pink stuffed amphibian, I jump to my feet.

"Rosie!" I hold my arms out, waiting to receive my axolotl. "I looked everywhere for her. I swore I lost it. Where did you find her?"

"It was in Rocco's room. I was cleaning up the last of everything and wanted to pull the bed back so I could shampoo the carpets. She was stuffed between the wall and his headboard. It looks like it was intentionally hidden." His voice lowers, but I still make out the last of his mutter, "stupid kid was always so jealous of you."

"Wow." I hug Rosie, remembering how it felt the first time North gave her to me, and I could have sworn that night he was going to ask me out.

He didn't.

Yet another example of how I thought he was shy, but he was merely being a nice guy. You'd think after all the chances that boy has had to ask me out, and he never has, he's just not interested.

Nobody is that shy.

I half smile, not feeling light enough for a full smile. I'm happy to have Rosie back, but in a way, it feels bittersweet. Part of me had hoped this gift had been more than a get-well gift, but I'm finally seeing that North never wanted to be with me. He was always just being a nice guy.

If he wanted to be with me, he would have said something by now.

Knock, knock, knock.

I jump to my feet and fly across the room because nobody uses the side door but North. As soon as I open the door, he exclaims, "You'll never guess what I just found!" He bursts over the threshold while waving papers in the air. "Oh, hi Mr. Bella." He tips his head toward Dad. "How are you?"

"I'm fine, son. What's all the commotion about?"

"You're not going to like this." His words take a cautionary tone as he plants his gaze on Dad. "Gia dropped off a box of Rocco's trophies at the school, and I got to putting them away tonight, and look." North slides papers in front of Dad. I peer over Dad's shoulder and gasp.

"What is this?" Clearly, I can read, but I don't believe it! "Is Rocco getting funding for his car lot in exchange for political favors?"

"It looks that way." North shifts his feet, as he keeps his gaze glued to Dad. "Did you know about this?"

"How could he know about that?" I scoff, but Dad blurts over the top of me.

"—I did." His eyelids lower, hooding his eyes, and his skin grows ashen. "Forgive me, but I found that box the other day, and that's why I had it sitting in the living room. I didn't have the heart to turn in my own son, but I know it needs to happen. I was hoping you'd come over, look in the box, and find it. Well, things didn't really go that way. When you offered to donate it to the school, I figured this would work out."

"Were you ever going to say anything?" Anger sizzles in my chest, not for Dad, because I oddly understand his plight, but at Rocco, who is about to drag our family through another scandal.

"I planned to send anonymous copies to the local press if you didn't find it. I also knew my heart can't handle the constant news and gossip, and that's the real reason I planned to go to Mexico." His head's still down, and I can't see his expression, but his voice is strong with conviction. "Rocco's a grown man who's made his own bed."

"If you'd like to avoid a mess with your own son, I can take this to the police myself," North offers. "He won't ever need to know you were going to turn him in. I know he's estranged now, but maybe some time in jail will help him to see things differently, and he won't blame you."

"I really don't think it will make a difference who turns him in but be my guest." Dad scratches at the back of his head, thinking through his words. "All I know is going through another one of these scandals with him is not on my Bingo card this year."

"It's not on my Bingo card either." A disgusted snort bleeps out of my mouth.

"You're welcome to come too." One corner of Dad's mouth curls at the tip as his gaze cuts to North. "But something tells me you have a reason to stay."

"I don't know if I do." With emotionally exhausted eyes, I turn to North. He seems to avoid my gaze, looking at the floor.

"I think that's my cue to leave you two." A gleam sparkles out of the corner of Dad's eye as he passes me on his way out of the kitchen, calling back, "I'm going to start packing my bags."

The silence that Dad's absence creates pulsates as I fix my gaze on North. *This has to be it.* We've been dancing around our connection for a decade. If North doesn't say something, then I'm going to. I can't wait another decade, wasting years we can be together.

And if I'm wrong about this?

Well, at least I will find out now.

"North." My voice cracks and I pause to swallow. "Dad asked if I have a reason to stay." I squawk out, so afraid of another disappointment. "Do I?"

"Do you?" North's dreamy eyes lock on me the same time his feet propel him across the room, closing the gap between us. He's so tall, he dips his head down to align our gazes, all his attention on me. "Gia, I've been in love with you from the first moment I saw you, but I couldn't tell you because Rocco threatened to destroy us both. I never wanted to cause any trouble for you. I held in my feelings all these years, wishing them away, but they only grew stronger." His eyes fill with tears, and his words float out like poetry, each word swelling my heart even more.

"I know you said it was too soon to decide what we are, but it's killing me. I need you to know that you're the only woman I've ever wanted."

His eyes bounce between my lips and my eyes, all the while his gaze becoming more heated, and the strongest magnetic pull of gravity I ever felt, draws me directly to his lips. We lean closer and closer, with each second ticking until our lips finally crash, instantly tangling as if we've been training to do this our whole lives. There isn't anything shy about the way he kisses me, or even polite. The chemistry is beyond anything I could have dreamed. We are perfectly matched to each other, and before I can take a deep breath, he pulls away, a boisterous smile covering his face.

"Mama Mia," I whisper, and fight back all the happy tears pricking the backs of my eyes.

"Mama Mia is right," Dad's voice echoes from the edge of the kitchen. Apparently, he used his snoopy manifesting power to sneak back down the hall and overhear our confessions. My laugh mingles with North's husky chuckle. I don't even care that Dad overheard us. It's not like any of this is a secret to him. He's the one who had called it all those years ago.

As the laughter dies, I gaze back at North. Talk about a truth bomb. It all makes so much sense now. I thought he was too shy, but he was protecting me from my own brother. After all this time, we can finally be honest with each other and be the couple we've always wanted to be.

"This calls for a celebration." Dad whoops from the corner.

"What's on your mind?" I turn back to Dad, enjoying how he's taking part in this whole thing. It's not the romantic declaration of love I dreamed about, with my dad in the corner, but in an odd way, it doesn't feel uncomfortable either.

"How about we go for one of those coffees you've been bringing over? My treat."

Pushing out my lower lip, I only need to muse for a second before I know I'm game. "Sounds good. North, what do you think?"

"Let's go."

"I'll drive." I lunge to steal my keys off the hook, before Dad can grab them, and race out in front of him.

Dad bursts out next, calling out, "Shotgun."

North laughs, as he pulls up the rear, shaking his head. "Maybe I should have been more careful about what I'm getting into," he teases while he climbs in the backseat of my car.

"It's fine. We aren't that scary. Just Dad's driving is awful. I couldn't let you experience that on top of everything else we've put you through." Nothing can erase the smile on my lips, as I gaze at him in the rearview mirror. On the drive over, Dad jokes about all the times he caught

North looking at me over the years, and North's ears grow a healthy shade of crimson. Before he starts revealing my secrets—because I know he caught me looking back at North—I pull over in front of the Coffee Loft and rush to get out.

North and I link hands, weaving our fingers together, and stroll through the Coffee Loft door with Dad in tow. Dad smack talks North from behind us "Tell me you're going to try something other than that stinky chai."

"What?" North jolts, turning back to fake scowl at Dad. "You did not just insult my drink order."

"I did. After all these years, you finally brewed up the courage to kiss Gia. It's time for you to turn a new leaf all together and try a new drink."

"What's going on here, chai guy?" Portia butts in, leaning over the counter with her gaze directly on North. "Are we seriously talking about not having chai?"

"I guess, I'm breaking my habits." North shrugs, and looks at me, his eyes glittering back with all the shades of dreamy, rich espresso. "I'll have whatever she's having."

"You got it." Portia's curious smile curves on her lips as she punches our order in, and we pay. Then we link arms, heading back to our booth, and slide in to sit shoulder to shoulder with Dad across from us. We aren't the couple of kids we were in high school. I can't say we're better off, just different. Our lives are actually fairly uneventful, which will leave us plenty of time for long dates at the Coffee Loft where we laugh, bond, and fall in love, one sloooow sip at a time.

TWENTY
A month later

As we survey the piles of remaining items in my dad's garage, North and I can't help but chuckle at the absurdity of some of them. First, there is a broken pizza oven that Dad swears still works. Before we packed it up to donate, he added a note saying, "Works, but cooks unevenly. It doesn't make the best tasting pizza, but it makes a fun conversation piece." I really just want to chuck that oven into the garbage, but getting rid of this stuff has been an emotional journey for Dad, and the only way he's made it through it is by believing his stuff will find a better home where people who need it, can use it.

My favorite item is the whole box of flamingo yard ornaments. I can't fathom why someone would ever need that many, but my childish brain wants to prank North by putting them in his yard one night.

Such innocent fun, but I resist.

Oh, and don't get me started on the hideous plastic garden gnomes. There are eleven of them. Who in their right mind needs that many lawn creatures? I would think if you had eleven, you'd actually want a full dozen, which leads me to think one is missing. Frankly, that's a little terrifying. I've learned to tiptoe around, hoping it doesn't pop out at me sometime. Their facial expressions are just too creepy.

I know it's silly.

But really, its creepy.

Now, we are down to the last load of stuff, and I couldn't help but rub my hand along the base of the old palm tree shaped lamp adorned in Christmas lights.

"Quite the assortment of stuff, eh?" North chuckles, his eyes wafting to the lamp, and I couldn't help but join in.

It is definitely a relief, after the last few weeks, to finally be able to laugh about this stuff. "Yeah, I think we can honestly say we have something for everyone."

"Too bad this violin doesn't have a bow. I'd definitely give you ten bucks for it." He picks up a small stringed instrument. Dad is always more eccentric, even in his collections, and I doubt that he had any classical instruments. I squint my eyes at North, and I burst out laughing.

"That's not a violin. It's a Ukulele, and it's definitely worth at least twenty bucks," I tease, pretending to be offended.

"Sorry." He put it back in the box with his fingers exaggeratedly spaced, as if he is now afraid to touch it. His expression takes on a bit of a conspiratorial gleam. "I have a surprise."

One of my brows rises higher than the other in a skeptical glare. "After reading the news article this morning about Rocco and his buddies and how detectives were able to bring to light even more closed-door embezzlement and fraud, I don't know if I can handle any more surprises."

"This has nothing to do with them. I actually think they are the only ones who are surprised they didn't get away with their scams for good. They will be in jail for a long time." He shakes his head, but continues with excitement inflections in his voice, "This is a good surprise. I was talking to your dad about Mexico. It turns out my parents aren't that far from Lake Xochimilco, the most popular place in North America for finding wild axolotls."

"Oh, I see where this is going." I pretend to be alarmed, but inside I'm already excited. "That's enticing, and you want to visit, right?"

"What do you think?" His head takes an inquisitive angle. "Both our parents are there, and maybe we could visit for Christmas? It would be our first vacation together, cementing another milestone in our still new relationship."

My heart patters over several beats as I love how thoughtful North is, and how willing he is to include me in his life, making plans for Christmas, which is a month away. It feels normal though. Like how it's supposed to be. "You're asking me if I want to go to Mexico in cold December? Of course, I would love to go."

"One more thing." His easy smile graces his face, but I freeze as a serious gleam sparkles out of the corner of his eye. "In the spirit of letting go, I cleaned out a few of my closets, too. I was going to toss this, but part of me always had this weird fantasy and I wanted to give it to you." He lifts up a box and pushes it toward me. "You'll like this one."

"Promise?" I hesitate, but lean over, peering inside the box. When I make out the contents, a full smile bursts on my lips. "Are you kidding me?" I yank it out, and eagerly slip it on. "You brought me your high school football letterman jacket?"

"I know we aren't in high school." He shifts his weight from one foot to the other, "But seeing you walk through the halls in my jacket was one of those things I always fantasized about. If only I would have been a little braver back then, we'd have a lot more memories." He pulls up one side of his mouth into a flirty grin. "So, what do you say, Gia Bella...I'm a little late but will you wear my lettermen jacket?

"Gosh, North." I playfully bat my lashes and tug on the collar hugging it closer around me, already loving everything about this jacket. The worn leather still smells amazing, and it's soft and so easy to mold against my skin. "If you want me to wear your jacket, that must mean I really am your girl?"

"That's exactly what you are to me." He leans in, stealing a chaste kiss from my lips, before tacking on, *"My Girl."*

That kiss isn't enough for either one of us. Our gaze lingers over each other, and he dips his chin again, pressing his lips against mine. This kiss is sweet and filled with the promise of something more. As we pull away, I see the same wonder in his eyes that I feel in my heart.

I tug the jacket even tighter around me, a warmth seeps into my chest, and I take one more look around the garage. I can't help but smile. It had been an overwhelming several weeks, but now that we'd gotten through all that junk, I know we have better things ahead.

Epilogue

Christmas in Mexico

The waves cascade gently on top of the water, creating a ripple that goes on as far as I can see. We're staying at North's parents' house, but I decided to take the day to visit the ocean as it's always been where I felt the calmest. For a moment, I'm sad as I reminisce about how I used to look out at the beach almost every day when I worked at the resort. Though I love working at Dad's pizzeria, it's not the same as having a career that's solely mine.

"What are you thinking about?" North walks barefoot beside me on our sunrise walk. His face is already sun-kissed even though we've only been here two days.

"Just how peaceful the ocean is, and how I miss working at the resort."

"Have you thought about what direction you want to go with your career after your dad returns to Bella's?"

"No." My mind is calm, and it doesn't pull me in any direction except to whatever direction is closest to North. "I know it wasn't in my plan to have a career change now, but I do think it's been the best thing that could have happened because these past few weeks of getting to spend so much time with you have been everything to me."

"I feel the same way." North takes my hand in his, and my heart melts how our fingers lace together so perfectly. "I hate to say I'm grateful you got laid off, but I've been selfishly enjoying all the late-night left-over pizza dinners together."

"Those are amazing, but my favorite is the daily Coffee Loft visits." I hold up a teasing finger. "Maybe, when we return, I'll try to get a job there?"

"That's actually not a bad idea." North's voice ticks up in excitement. "I saw a Help Wanted sign in the window before we left. It's right across the street from the Pizzeria. You can see your dad all the time, but still have your own space, and room for upward advancement. I know Portia and Christian so well, I'm sure they'd hire you."

"Maybe." I purse my lips out, mulling over the idea. The sun is rising higher over the horizon, casting a warm glow over the water, making everything tranquil. "I do have my Food Manager's License already, and I enjoy that type of work."

"It would be perfect." North gushes, and everything suddenly feels perfect. North is the man of my dreams, the one I've been hoping for my whole life. Now that we're together, he's not only the sweetest guy ever, but so supportive in every way. Getting laid off could have been stressful, but it just seems like things work out better and better now that he's by my side.

"I really appreciate how supportive you've been with me." I halt and look deeply into his eyes. North never had one those piercing gazes you read about in romance novels. His is the kind of warm intensity that brings so much familiarity, I'm always left feeling like I had known North not just since my youth, but for a thousand lifetimes.

North reaches for my other hand, pulling both of my hands to his heart. This is honestly my favorite thing he does, and it makes my heart skip a beat every time. His chest rises and lowers in the deepest breath as I stand before him, my eyes searching his face for what feels like an eternity. And then, with a rasp in his voice, he finally says, "I don't know if this is too soon or not, but I can't hold it in anymore. I love you, Gia."

His declaration echoes in the air between us, as if suspended by the salty wind. A gentle smile tugs at the corners of my lips, and I squeeze his hands back. "I love you too," I whisper, my voice surprisingly cracking as I felt the weight of these words I'd never said to any man wash over me like the waves lapping at my bare feet. And in that moment, we stand on the sandy shore with nothing but the sound of the ocean. I have no clue where I'm going in life but I don't care. I just want to grow closer to North as I finally found someone special – My *one true North.*

Bonus Epilogue

"Welcome to the Coffee Loft." I adjust my apron, clear my throat, and bat my lashes over the counter at the handsome man waiting to be served. It's my first day on the job, working as a new assistant manager, and I already know I'm going to love everything about working for Coffee Loft. "How can I help you?"

"I'm not sure yet." North leans over on the counter, resting both elbows. "Whatever I get I'm going to need a Lofty size as the car wash is just beginning, and I have a feeling it's going to be a long day."

"That's right." I slowly press the buttons on the tablet to punch in a Lofty size drink, making sure I don't miss anything. "How many players do you think will show up to help out?"

"I made it a required practice, so it better be the whole team. We have to earn money some way."

"Oh, before I forget." I grab his coffee cup but rest it in my palm as I have so many thoughts racing through my brain. "Did my dad get ahold of you for the final count of pizzas you need donated? I think he was going to do about thirty. Is that okay?"

"That should be phenomenal. I hate fundraising, but every little bit helps."

Portia walks forward, smiling sweetly toward North. "Why don't you put Coffee Loft down for donating some gift cards for the auction."

"That's awfully sweet of you." North nods, pulling his phone out to make a note. "I'm messaging our secretary now before I forget to add it to the roster." After a moment of typing, he looks back up from his phone. "Boy, there's so much to remember with these things, but it's coming together. We'll have football for at least another year."

"That's the goal, right?" Another customer passes through the front door, and I hate to rush North, but I'm super slow at making drinks, and I hate to get behind. "Did you want your chai?"

"What do you think?" North beams at me as his gaze paces from me to Portia, who quietly stands behind me to assist with my training. "Should I go back to my usual chai, or find something new?"

"You know what I think." I playfully hold off to wait for that sparkle in his eye that always appears when I tease him.

"What's that?" He leans one arm on the counter, and I marvel how his arms get better looking every day.

My heart blooms full of so much love as I know I finally found my place. I love my new life, working at the Coffee Loft. I get to see Dad most days as he's only across the street, and I love that I'm finally living my days with North. Nothing else matters. "I don't care if you order pumpkin spice, vanilla or chai. The only thing I care about is that you are *my guy*."

Thank you for reading No More Mr. Chai Guy.

Just a note to say, if you enjoyed Rocco being a villain, he returns in The Pucker-Up Pact.

The Pucker-Up Pact is a grumpy sunshine, revenge fake-dating, sweet romantic comedy with a HEA.

Instant Chemistry

Revenge Fake Dating

Forced Proximity

She's Mine Vibes

If you haven't read it yet, it's available in KU.

Welcome back to The Coffee Loft,

where a new round of stories has been brewed especially for you.

Those of you stopping by to visit again, we've missed you. The feeling of home is the same that you loved before.

If it's your first time, prepare
to be swept off your feet.

While our menu hasn't changed, we think you'll be pleased
with the fall favorites we've added. Fans of pumpkin spiced
lattes, peppermint mochas, and rich, chocolaty cocoas
will not be disappointed. This multi-author collection of
stand-alone sweet romcoms is filled to the brim with the
swoons you love and adore.

From sweet kisses to grand gestures and matchmaking surprises, each mug and story will be filled with everything
you crave. So come on in and let us
serve you with that happy ever after you've come to expect.

Find the entire collection here: https://www.amazon.co
m/dp/B0CXQBFPHK
　　While you are at it, visit the first collection here:
https://www.amazon.com/dp/B0CG2MQP2J

Sneak Peek

Let's Not and Sleigh We Did - Coming October 2024.

Oh, oh, the mistletoe, hung where I did NOT see.

My brother's friend waits for me and gets down on one knee— *What is happening?*

Somebody stop it, please!

Oh, those dreamy blue eyes batting at me, and all the words he dares to say

This is bad

Like really, really bad

We're now planning a wedding day

But it's all for a good reason, *not love*

Oh, cough, cough, let's not bust out the L-word

It's purely business

It is a solid plan until it isn't

So maybe I love him, but we agreed not to do that
. . . whoops

Let's Not and Sleigh We Did is a fake mar-
riage of convenience, brother's best friend, *just-kiss-
es-but-all-the-swoons* Romcom

It's up for preorder now at an introductory price.
https://www.amazon.com/dp/B0DF1PB7DY

Also by J.P. Sterling

<u>Christmas Shenanigans</u> (All Standalones)

Mingle All the Way

Tis the Season to Get Married

Let's Not and Sleigh We Did (Coming Oct 2024)

<u>The Coffee Loft Series</u> (All Standalones)

Pardon My French Press

No More Mr. Chia Guy

<u>Sweet Hockey RomCom</u> (All Standalones)

The Pucker-Up Pact

Shot Through the Heart (Coming 2025)

<u>A Modern Fairy Tale Series</u> (All Standalones)

Royally Rugged

Royally Guarded (Coming Spring 2025)

***Bosses and Billionaires Series* (<u>All Standalones</u>)**

Maid for my Billionaire Boss

Upcycling My Rig-Pig Boss

Kissed by My Billionaire Boss

Marooned with My Celebrity Boss

A Heart that Dances Series

Dancing on Broken Ankles

The Stars We See

A Heart that Dances

A Heart that Loves

Water and Stone Duet

Ruby in the Water

Lily in the Stone

About J.P. Sterling

J.P. Sterling grew up watching old reruns of Lucille Ball and Mary Tyler Moore and fell in love with wholesome entertainment and slapstick comedy. She loves leaning into the over-the-top humor and full circle moments, especially if it means the underdog gets to shine.

Aside from writing, she's also a wife and homeschooling mom, a holistic dietitian, a former college professor and lover of all-things dark chocolate.

*No swears. Just kisses. No Blasphemies. *

Let's get social!

Hey you amazing reader! You are invited to join my private reader group for all-things clean books and friends. Enter the group here: https://www.facebook.com/groups/15008507640081965

Other places to follow me:

Instagram: https://www.instagram.com/stories/authorjpsterling/

Facebook: https://www.facebook.com/jpsterlingauthor/

Amazon: https://www.amazon.com/stores/author/B01N9TJXJN/about

Acknowledgements

With every book I write, my list of people who have found their way into my path just keeps growing, and it's impossible to thank everyone. It's truly the best problem to have.

I first thank God, who gave me this mission to write clean books. I never in a million years thought I'd have these many books (20!). I seriously was going to write only one as a bucket list thing.

Always, I thank you, amazing readers and everyone in the book world. It's an honor to have a corner in this space.

Brooks is always on top on the list because he helps me plot everything out, and I really couldn't do this writing thing without him.

My team of editors and proofreaders. I have so many amazing readers who don't hesitate to send me screenshots of all the little missed words or extra spaces. It seriously takes a whole village for me to write a book, and I'm so thankful for mine. A special shout to Natalie this round.

For Amy, my Coffee Loft copilot, and all my fellow Coffee Loft authors! This set was never on my radar. It started as a serendipitous event of accidentally designing the cover concept with Amy. We took that concept and started playing with titles, and we just knew we had to bring it life. It has been the most fun labor of love I've done in my writing career, and I'm grateful everyone is plugging along with us.

My family – *hearts to infinity.*